Spark a Story

Spark a Story

Twenty Short Stories by American Teens

Selected by the Editors of
Houghton Mifflin Harcourt

HOUGHTON MIFFLIN HARCOURT

BOSTON • NEW YORK   2017

For information about permission to reproduce selections from this book, write to trade.permissions@hmhco.com or to Permissions, Houghton Mifflin Harcourt Publishing Company, 3 Park Avenue, 19th Floor, New York, New York 10016.

www.hmhco.com

Library of Congress Cataloging-in-Publication Data is available.

ISBN 978-1-328-88197-7

Printed in the United States of America

DOC 10 9 8 7 6 5 4 3 2 1

"A Sixth Sense" copyright © 2017 by Tal Bajaroff

"Undoing Reality" copyright © 2017 by Kayla Bernhoester

"The Gene" copyright © 2017 by Jaryn Blair

"Silent Words" copyright © 2017 by Niki Borghei

"The Sickle" copyright © 2017 by Carlo Di Bernardo

"The Unfortunate Tale of Sam Withersby" copyright © 2017 by Kyla Duhart

"Dream World" copyright © 2017 by Adelle Else

"Noli Me Tangere" copyright © 2017 by Bethany Hall

"Only a Fool Would" copyright © 2017 by Aamna Haq

"Of Metaphors, Monsters, and Wild Thoughts" copyright © 2017 by Annie Hoang

"Arasing" copyright © 2017 by Morgan Levine

"All Westbound Trains" copyright © 2017 by Simon Liu

"A Portrait of the Artist as a Teenage Girl" copyright © 2017 by Aela Morris

"The Cabin" copyright © 2017 by Rushalee Nirodi

"Etiam Doloris" copyright © 2017 by Joshua Peck

"Squish" copyright © 2017 by Hannah Perry

"Black and White" copyright © 2017 by Victoria Richardson

"The Letters" copyright © 2017 by Destiny Trinh

"Sunday" copyright © 2017 by Grace Twomey

"The Flood" copyright © 2017 by Amelia Van Donsel

Contents

Introduction

FOR OVER A HUNDRED YEARS Houghton Mifflin Harcourt has published annual editions of *The Best American Short Stories,* a collection culled from a wide range of publications, in a two-step process. First, a series editor—in recent years, Heidi Pitlor—reads everything she can get her hands on, and picks about one hundred contenders. She removes the author names and any other identifying information and sends them to a guest editor (a different, well-known writer each year), who makes a final selection of twenty-odd choices. These collections have been so successful for so long that they have inspired a number of parallel volumes: *The Best American Essays, The Best American Sports Writing, The Best American Comics,* et al.

At the same time, through the decades, HMH has been a leading publisher of preschool and elementary- and secondary-school educational materials. So it may come as a surprise that we have only now come up with a simple idea: Could we take our experience with the Best American series and combine it with our contacts at every high school in the country, in order to inspire students to enter a short story competition?

Here's how it worked:

- The competition was open to all high school students in the United States.
- Hundreds of entries were read independently by three HMH judges, after author names and identifying information were removed.

- Entries were judged on creativity, originality, and overall quality of writing.
- The fifty strongest entries were presented to our team of fiction editors to make a final selection of the top twenty.

This team comprised ten men and women who read fiction submissions for a living, and who have helped HMH publish award-winning and beloved novels and story collections for many years. They really enjoyed the chance to read these young writers' efforts. Speaking as one member, I can report that it was refreshing to have the chance to peer inside the minds of younger, developing writers, young men and women who might not yet have mastered all aspects of their craft but were experimenting with voice, character, and world building.

There were a certain number of realistic coming-of-age stories—no surprise there—but there were a large number of science fiction and crime stories, too, and even some horror stories (though not so many that we worried about the psychological state of America's youth).

The winning entries have been copyedited for style and usage, and (as with any of our Best American collections) they vary widely in subject, tone, and setting. Collectively, they give us reasons to be hopeful about the next generation of American writers and storytellers. Here are twenty creative young minds at work, at least some of whom will surely go on to write full-length novels and perhaps screenplays, too. Enjoy.

BRUCE NICHOLS, publisher
Houghton Mifflin Harcourt

Spark a Story

TAL BAJAROFF

A Sixth Sense

IT SMELLED OF DAMP SOCKS. I usually enjoy the smell, but today something was off. The surrounding atmosphere seemed to close in on me. I snuggled further into my bed. The smell was pungent. What was about to happen? The last time I experienced this was too long ago for me to remember the outcome. My roommate called me from across the house. Excited to see her, I quickly jumped out of bed and sprinted to her. All sorts of questions started swirling in my head: *What time is it? What are we going to eat? Are we going to go for a run? Is that new?*

But then I remembered that's not what I really wanted to know. I glanced over only to find a darkening sky. Was it already night? My roommate had no answers for my questions. She just looked at me and smiled.

After we finished the season finale of our favorite show, there was a flash of light followed by a booming sound that resonated within the house. This raised the hairs on the back of my neck.

I leaped from the couch and ran to the window only to find it was raining. *Of course! A storm!* I should have known. As I trotted back to the couch to inform my roommate about the downpour, someone rang the doorbell. This diverted my attention away from the storm. My roommate and I proceeded to the door. More questions arose in my head: *Who's at the door? Will we be going on that run? What's that smell? Who's at the door?* Once again I regained my focus. A tall, lanky figure walked through the door and greeted my roommate with a warm embrace, pushing me aside. They briskly walked out the door, leaving me behind.

A few hours passed. The storm had died down and I could hear the clattering of keys opening the apartment door. *She's back!* I rushed to greet my roommate. She bent down to pet me. "I'm sorry, Duke," she said. My tail began to wag as she reached for the leash. As the rain ceased to fall, we stepped out onto the paved sidewalk and finally went on the run to the dog park that I had been dreaming about all day.

Undoing Reality

IN EVERY DIRECTION there was nothing but sand. I was alone. I squinted up at the sun; its harsh rays pierced my pale skin through the cloudless sky. It was completely silent. The sand, oddly enough, didn't burn my bare feet. In fact, it almost felt cold. I felt a wave of heat roll through my entire body, immediately followed by a stronger wave of ice as my heart forced its way into my throat and made it difficult to breathe. I covered my eyes and screamed as loudly as I possibly could in an attempt to allow myself to breathe again. Even after I ran out of breath, my anxiety continued to grow. I ran my hands through my hair, squeezing my eyelids together. I was completely lost in a foreign place with no memory of why I was there and no clue how I would get home.

Home . . . Do I even know where home is?

I felt a hand on my shoulder. I uncovered my eyes and saw glossy marbled water that danced with the sun on the concrete walls. My feet were dipped in the cool water, and the warm sun was beating down on my shoulders.

"Jessica! I know the water's cold, but that's really no reason to shout," my mother's voice playfully scolded behind me. I turned myself around to see her holding a tray with three tall glasses that had a pale yellow liquid in them, in the hand she didn't have resting on my tense shoulder.

"I was gardening when I saw the lemons were ripe, so I thought I'd make us some lemonade." She grinned, taking a glass and holding it out to me.

I smiled down at the pale liquid, watching the translucent flowers bob up and down. I smiled at the thought of my five-foot-two-inch mother climbing the ten-foot tree to gather lemons. Though, this wasn't really surprising. She loved to do anything she possibly could to make me happy.

This included giving me little pointless things like flower-shaped ice cube trays. She loved to laugh with me about her silly impulse buys. I think that was the reason she bought that stuff: to see me smile. I could feel her looking at me as she admired my reaction to the flower-shaped ice cubes.

"Aren't they so cute?" my mother cheesed.

I smiled like I was listening, but I was completely lost in thought. Even though the event had passed, I debated telling my mother what I'd really been screaming about, but I didn't want to risk her thinking I was losing my mind over something so silly. Besides, I probably had just fallen asleep in the sun. It was very relaxing, after all. The smell of chlorine was emitting from the pool, and the breeze provided a beautiful relief from the sun that steadily grew hotter as the day aged. I could smell the hundreds of flowers that were clumped in my mom's garden, and I heard the gentle humming of fat, fuzzy bumblebees as they stuck their faces into the center of each grouping of petals.

I glanced over at my mother, who had seated herself in the beach chair she used specifically for the pool. People always said we looked alike, and I always took this as a compliment. A large pair of sunglasses currently covered her kind, blue eyes, and her dirty-blond hair was contained by one of those giant monster-toothed hairclips she loved to wear in the summer. Her two-piece dark-blue swimsuit exposed only a few inches of her stomach, though if she wanted to she could have pulled off a more exposing suit. Despite being forty-five, she still retained a thin, delicate figure. She was holding a book in her hand, and the tray with the two remaining lemonades sat on the small plastic table next to her.

I grinned when I saw she still had the black-and-purple yarn friendship bracelet I had made for her in the third grade tied around her wrist. This shouldn't have come as a shock; she still had my sloppy hand-turkeys from kindergarten hanging in the family room.

I dipped my feet deeper into the water so it dampened just the bottom of my rolled-up jeans, staring at the strange angles that the optical illusion of moving water created.

"Is that third glass of lemonade for Dad?" I asked, still staring at my feet.

"What third glass?" I heard my mother ask, honest confusion in her voice.

I turned to see my mom set the glass she was just drinking out of back onto an otherwise empty tray.

That's weird . . . I'm sure I saw three glasses . . .

"Oh, never mind." I paused. "When does Dad get off work?"

"He actually just called about an hour ago and told me he picked up another shift, so he'll be a few hours late. He also said something about a science project you needed help with. He said he'd be home as soon as he could, but to get a head start on it."

I sighed, the memory of my science project sticking in my conscience. Self-loathing boiled in my stomach as I harassed myself for procrastinating on something worth so many points. I stood up and began walking toward the glass screen door that led inside from the patio, when it suddenly disappeared.

Actually, everything disappeared.

The only thing left was a solid white color. I couldn't move. I couldn't speak. My head felt like it was going to explode and a queasy feeling began to spread along the lining of my stomach. Calm, muffled voices were interrupted by high-pitched screeching noises, which seemed to excite the voices dramatically. Blurry shadows began to move across my vision, and a dark shadow grew larger directly to my left. A deep, mature voice seemed to come out of it. I strained to listen.

He talked for what felt like hours, but I could only understand the last five words he said:

"Come back to me, Jess."

"Dad?" I gasped, but it was too late. Just as quickly as it began, it was over.

I was staring directly into a mirror. Sinks were lined side-by-side along the entire wall, but only the one in front of me had the water on. A pile of foam was cupped into my right hand, and all of the stalls behind me had the doors cracked open. I cautiously lowered my hands into the sink and washed them off, continuously glancing into the mirror. I cupped my hands in the cold water and splashed the cold liquid on my face. I sighed and shut my eyes.

"I'm not crazy. I'm *not* crazy. Okay, how did I get here?"

But for some reason I already knew the answer. I vividly remembered walking into the restaurant with my mother. She had a red dress on that nicely complemented her freshly tanned skin. She had told the pale waiter she wanted a table for two, and he asked if a booth would suit us, in a thick Russian accent. My mother told him that would be fine, so he walked us to our table. When I sat down, I could feel that the faux leather seat was cold through my black leggings, and I decided to put on the hoodie I had carried in with me. The waiter, who introduced himself as Lucas, gave us our menus and told us he'd bring us some waters. He then left us alone to decide what food we would like to order. After a short time of discussion, we'd decided to share a lobster as a special treat. Lucas returned with the two waters, and my mother told him what we wanted. He nodded and returned to the kitchen to bring us the lobster. I decided that I'd wash my hands while he was gone, so I excused myself to the bathroom. That's how I had gotten there.

So why do I also remember simply appearing here? What was that white vision I had? Was that real, or is this real? How could I have two different memories leading to the same scenario?

I pulled a paper towel out of the wall-mounted dispenser and dried my hands and face, readying myself to go back out to my mother.

I walked over to the table, and it was exactly how I had remembered it. My mother was still in her red dress, and the booth still felt cold when I sat down.

"Are you okay? You seem upset," my mother prodded, her eyebrows raised with worry.

"Yeah, I guess," I began to say, denying anything strange had even happened. "Or maybe not. I don't know."

"What's going on?"

I paused.

"Well," I started to say, but then I stopped. "It's probably nothing."

My mom pursed her lips like she always does when she's putting a lot of effort into what she's thinking.

"Is your medicine acting up? The doctors said there were side effects . . ."

Medication? I sat back in my seat, remembering the trip to the doctor's office from last week.

I was sitting on the bed in the white room. My mother was in one of the army-green chairs directly in front of me, my father in the other.

"We do have an experimental drug, and its effects could begin working within the first few hours of taking the pill," the woman in the white doctor's coat told me.

"What are the side effects?" my father inquired. I could tell he wasn't completely onboard with the whole "experimental drug" idea.

"Well, as of right now, the only official side effects are nausea and headaches. But there have been some reports of memory loss and mild confusion."

Mild confusion? That was probably a little under-exaggerated.

But in that moment in time, I couldn't remember why I had wanted to take that pill so badly.

"Jessie? Are you okay?"

My mother's voice once again brought me back into reality. The lobster was sitting on the table in front of us, a rich aroma emanating from the dead crustacean. My mother had already begun to dig some of the meat out of the shell.

"Yeah, I'm fine." I paused. "Hey, Mom, when did the lobster get here?"

"You were zoning out, dear. Would you like the tail?" she asked cheerfully, dropping the tail's meat onto my plate.

I stared at the pale meat and then back at my mother.

"I'm not really sure I'm hungry right now . . . Do you think we could just get a to-go box or someth—"

I heard a crash behind me. I turned around to see a tray flipped over on the stone tiles. A mixture of broken dinnerware and spilled food was heaped on the floor next to the table of a middle-aged married couple. Their attention was still focused on each other, and they seemed unaffected by the spilled food below them.

I turned back to my mother, who also seemed indifferent.

"What just happened?" I asked my mother.

"What?"

I stared blankly at my mother.

She had to have seen it. She's facing that direction, she had to see it!

"Excuse me, I believe you have a phone call in the back?" a new waiter interrupted. His eyes bounced around the room and he refused to make eye contact with me. If that wasn't already weird enough, he had his arms awkwardly forced into an L shape as if he was carrying something.

I looked at my mother, but she acted like she didn't even notice he was there. I cautiously got up and followed the waiter into the back room. The waiter was still holding his arms in the L shape and he was walking very oddly. His steps looked forced and awkward, like he was a video game character from the '90s. We went to the back office I assumed belonged to the head chef, and I picked the corded telephone up off of the counter and held it to my ear. A man's voice immediately began speaking.

"Please, we've been trying to reach you for years. Something went wrong. Please, if you can hear me, you need to get away from your mothe—"

Silence.

"Hello? Who is this? Is this a prank call?"

Silence.

"This isn't funny. Answer me! Who's there?"

The silence was replaced by startlingly loud static. I ripped the phone off of my ear and stared at it while it continued to whine in my hand.

I cautiously placed the phone back on its receiver and walked back to my mother, passing the strange waiter and the couple with the spilled food next to their table. The mess was gone and cleaned up nicely, but the couple were acting oddly. They seemed to be attempting to eat off of invisible plates with their silverware.

Crazy loves company, I guess.

"Where did you disappear to?" my mother asked as I sat back down across from her. She casually dipped a shrimp into the bowl of deep red cocktail sauce before taking a bite.

I paused, staring at her.

"I had a phone call," I slowly explained, "but I think it was just a prank call."

She saw everything that just happened, right? I couldn't have walked away from the table without her noticing . . .

She nodded and continued eating the shellfish.

"Wait . . ." I stared at her plate. "When did you order shrimp?"

"What are you talking about, Jessica? We ordered shrimp to share."

"No, we ordered a lobster to share," I cautiously argued.

"It's just your medication acting up again," my mother insisted, shrugging it off.

Heat began to fester in my cheeks as my body turned hot with anger and embarrassment. I took a deep breath, rubbing my eyes as if that would calm me down and make me understand what was happening. I dug my palms into my eyes until I saw blue and purple galaxies sparkling in my head. Suddenly I removed my hands. I had remembered something important.

"Mom, where's Dad?"

My mother pursed her lips and nervously adjusted her dress.

"Sweetheart, you don't remember?"

I shook my head unsurely, but a horrible feeling burned in my stomach.

"Your father," she said, starting to tear up, "he died in a car accident two years ago. He's gone . . . I'm so sorry, Jessie."

My face whitened. This couldn't be right. He was just late coming home from work yesterday—or was that just another mistake of my memory?

Anger and confusion snaked through my body. My chest felt cold and tingly, almost numb. I couldn't feel myself breathe, but I didn't really care if I was. Pressure began to build in my head, and I slammed my hands into the table. Standing up, I stormed off. I heard my mom yell after me, but her words didn't matter.

I can't handle this. I can't.

I had to go on a walk to clear my head, but as soon as I stomped through the front door, everything went white again.

The mechanical high-pitched sound was louder than ever. It shocked spikes into my brain with every noise. I heard a panicked, squeaky female's voice this time.

"We're losing her!"

I saw fuzzy shadows that looked like they could be people rushing around me. I tried to speak, but nothing would come out.

Why can't I speak to them?

The whiteness turned to blackness, and I opened my eyes to see a pitch-black sky littered with stars.

"Come on," a deep, familiar voice coaxed me as a hand appeared in my line of view. I took it, and the hand's owner pulled me onto my feet.

I saw the silhouette of a man holding a fishing pole and a tackle box. He held the pole out to me, and I could see the moonlight reflecting off of his teeth as he grinned.

"You wanted to learn how to fish, right?"

I cautiously took the pole.

"You alright, Jess?" he asked me.

Dad! He's my dad.

I bit my tongue, trying to think of the right words to say.

"Dad," I said. "I, uh . . . I had a dream that you died."

I stared out at the water layered with glitter under the moonlight.

"What? You had a dream that I—" My dad coughed, making mock-choking sounds and wrapping his hands around his throat before laughing his deep, hearty laugh.

I rolled my eyes and laughed with him.

God, I hate his jokes.

"I think your medication might be acting up again, yeah? So, do you remember how we got here?"

I thought for a moment. We had climbed all the way up this cliff because I told him I wanted to learn how to fish. My dad had never fished a day in his life, but he'd kick himself if he missed out on a chance to bond with me. He carried the two brand-new fishing poles paired with a fully stocked tackle box, and I lugged his backpack there. He looked at it as a learning experience for the both of us. He was wearing an army-green hat riddled with holes from being overworn. The words RESPECT MY AUTHORITY were written in all caps around a small round figure wearing sunglasses in the center. He was wearing his father's fishing vest, and he bragged about his twenty-two pockets during the whole car ride here.

"I have one pocket for every Trump supporter!" he had shouted while we were getting worms in Walmart, upsetting the old cashier. We had laughed about it while we walked back to his truck in the parking lot.

"Yeah, I remember," I said, focusing on his silhouette.

"Good, that's good. Alright, let's fish!" he said as he clapped his hand on the back of my neck and rubbed my shoulder.

"As long as you put the worms on. They're way too slimy for me." I scrunched up my face, causing a warm chuckle from my father.

He pulled a radio out of his backpack, still grinning. He turned on the radio, and "Blackbird" by the Beatles began playing from the speaker.

"Ah, the Beatles. My favorite," my dad grinned, sitting down in the dewy grass. "Okay, so you're gonna want to make sure your line is behind you, and to cast, I think you press down the button and—"

The music changed to static. Startled, I stared at the radio. A woman's voice spoke between fits of white noise.

"Shouldn't—woken up?—wear off—coma ward—get—off medication—with—father—get them out—not fair to the kid—depression—wakes up—What do you mean nothing's working?—need to wake up."

The radio began to play music again.

"What the hell was that?" I asked my dad.

"What?" my dad said, his attention on his orange glow-in-the-dark bobber down in the water below us.

"No, you had to hear that! The radio just had some kind of voice coming out of it, I swear. They said something about—"

"Jess, I think you need to clear your head. Here, I'll turn off the radio. Why don't you cast your line?" my dad directed, his face full of concern.

I took my royal-blue pole from him and waited for my father to put the oozing worm on the hook. I would usually make a comment about how gross it was, but my mind was elsewhere as I stared at the impaled but still wiggling worm.

"Oh, it doesn't bother me," my dad laughed.

I looked away from the worm to stare inquisitively at my father.

"I didn't say anything," I insisted, though I wasn't completely sure.

Could I have just forgotten I said anything? No, there's no way.

"Maybe I'm going crazy," he said with mock seriousness before breaking into a huge grin.

I lightly laughed with him before casting my line and staring into the open water. I became lost in my thoughts.

Am I going crazy? What did that girl on the radio say? "Wake up!" Wake up? Wake up from what? I am awake! Aren't I? It's probably just

*another fluke of my medication. My medication . . . What am I tak-
ing this for? Why do I need this medication so badly? Oh God . . . Oh
God . . .*

I swung my feet over the side of the cliff, gripping the fishing
rod in my hands until my knuckles glowed white in contrast to
the solid black night. My breath quickened and I clenched my
jaw. I stared hard at the waves crashing into the rocks below me
in an attempt to calm my nerves.

"Hey, Dad, why am I taking this medicine? What is it for?"
I asked. When I didn't get a response, I turned around to see
that my dad wasn't there. His tackle box, his radio, *everything* had
just . . . disappeared. I slowly looked back to the ocean and . . .

There's no way . . .

The fishing rod I had been using for the past hour was missing
from my hands.

Suddenly it was silent. The waves crashing under my feet had
become still. I licked my lips and felt the pressure in my chest
steadily build.

I'm crazy. I am completely crazy.

Behind me I heard deep laughter followed by something
being unzipped. My shoulders tensed, and I snapped my head
around to see my dad taking his radio out of his backpack, laughing at my surprise.

"Did I scare you?" he said with a grin.

My shoulders relaxed a bit, but I was still confused.

*Did he pack everything up just to play a joke on me? No . . . that
wouldn't make sense. None of this is making any sense!*

Tears began to well up in my eyes. It was too much. I stared
back out at the water. It was so beautiful, a perfect serenity to
battle my heightening anxiety. The deep-purple abyss swirled
under my feet as the surface shimmered under the moonlight.
The water's breath fogged the air, and I breathed it in. With every breath, the intake of oxygen became more difficult. Soon I
wouldn't be able to breathe.

I heard my dad finally get the radio to work behind me, and a
familiar tune began to play.

Didn't this already happen?

"Ah, the Beatles. My favorite," I heard my dad say again.

The burning in my throat suddenly cooled. My anxiety melted

away. I was completely numb. I stared straight ahead at nothing, my eyes glossing over.

I took a deep breath, letting the music fill my brain. I shut my eyes and scooted forward on the ledge before pushing myself off into the abyss.

I open my eyes to a solid white hospital room. Busy people in white lab coats who are various ages and various genders surround me, and they are all staring. I look to my right and see a monitor displaying an identical monitor . . . which showed another of the same monitor . . .

Oh, God. Could they see everything I saw?

I touch my hand to my forehead and feel the various wires stuck there. In a fit of panic, I rip them off of my head, and the monitor goes black.

"Where the *hell* am I?" I demand, unaffected by the dozen doctors surrounding my white bed.

The doctors stare at each other, clearly unsure who should explain. A janitor pushes his cart, stacked with spray bottles, paper towels, mops, and more. He seems not to notice the intensity clouding the air.

Finally, a middle-aged man with graying hair cautiously steps forward.

"You're in Berthen Laboratories. You agreed to partake in an experimental drug trial on account that it allowed you to see your parents again."

"My parents? Why? What happened to my parents?"

The doctors exchange sympathetic glances.

"Your parents"—a young female doctor bites her lip uncomfortably as she searches for the right wording—"*passed* . . . when you were about four years old. This drug trial . . . It granted you the opportunity to speak with them again, but it didn't work out quite as well as we had hoped."

I sit in silence, staring at the sympathetic faces, each refusing to break eye contact, as if they could find the answers to their questions in my eyes.

"We saw everything you saw," a young Asian doctor squeaks, pushing back her glasses. "What made you jump?"

Each of the doctors are staring at me in anticipation of my

answer. At that moment, an acoustic guitar begins to play over the hospital radio.

> *Blackbird fly, Blackbird fly*
> *into the light of the dark black night.*

The janitor moves to the window and stares outside, abandoning his cart in the corner of the room. He suddenly turns around and faces me, his arms still in front of him as if he is pushing his cart. His radio begins to produce static. "—she can't really believe—won't listen to—need to get—out of there—"

The janitor returns to his cart and pulls out a blue spray bottle and a towel. He sprays the table under the window and begins to clean as if nothing had ever happened.

I look out the window to see the roof of the industrial building next to Berthen Laboratories. The frame is unlocked, and the bottom of the window is cracked open, whispering to me.

Beckoning to me . . .

I don't know what's real anymore.

JARYN BLAIR

The Gene

TODAY WAS MY BIRTHDAY. I was turning seventeen and I hated it. I wished I had the gene. I wanted to experience it, even just once. I got to see it happen, of course, got to watch it happen to my friends. We learned about it in science class, we learned how it worked. I couldn't understand what was wrong with me. No one else could either. The doctors just said it was a birth defect and it was bound to happen. But if it were a birth defect, I would have met someone else or at least heard about someone else who didn't have it. No, instead it just earned me a lifetime of bullying and confused faces.

"Yo, man, you okay?" my friend asked, cutting me from my trance.

"Oh yeah, fine," I said, turning to face him.

"You sure?" he asked. I nodded. He didn't know I didn't have the gene and I really didn't intend on having him find out yet.

"Yeah, I'm sure, look I gotta go. My mom needs me," I stated.

"It's your birthday!" my friend exclaimed. I shrugged my shoulders.

We talked for a couple more minutes before I finally managed to get away from him and go home.

"Hey, honey!" my mom called from the kitchen when I walked in.

"Hey," I said, slinging my bag to the floor and walking into the kitchen, grabbing a granola bar from the pantry.

"Happy birthday," my mom said, moving to hug me.

"No, Mom, please don't," I stated and stepped backward, not wanting to have the same conversation we'd had last year, and the year before, and the one before that.

She sighed. "Honey, just because you don't have the cloning gene doesn't mean you can't age," she said a lot quieter and took a step toward me. Yep, this conversation was going to happen again.

"You're right, I don't have the cloning gene, so therefore I age differently than everyone else. I can die sooner, I can get in accidents, there's so many things that can happen to me where I can die!" I yelled and turned, going upstairs, not wanting the conversation to go further. I knew how it ended. It was the same thing every single year for as long as I could remember.

The cloning gene is what kept us alive, kept us from making mistakes. We could have the perfect life, get as many redos as we wanted. I'd seen my friend. He used to be a year older than me but he accidentally drove his car off a cliff in a midnight joyride. Now he was a year younger than me. My uncle had shot three people when he was forty-one. He got caught and was found guilty at forty-three. Now he's forty again. He never shot those people. He was younger than the shooter and besides, everyone was still okay, yeah, they might be younger but they were okay. And my uncle hadn't shot them yet. He'd done it with the forty-one-year-old body. The forty-two- and forty-three-year-olds faced the consequences of that. But the forty-year-old body? That body hadn't shot anyone, so he was okay.

Me? I had to live with what I got. I got no do-overs; whatever mistakes I made, I had to live with. I couldn't see how far down the lake a few miles north of here went down. The bottomless lake, as we called it. Everyone else could go down to the bottom with no fear of drowning and dying. Me? I couldn't do that. I had to be careful. Anything could kill me. People used to be like me; well, I guess they did, that's what I learned in history at least, but now no one was like me. One specialist said maybe evolution was reverting back to how it used to be. Another one said it was just a glitch in our system. I didn't know who to believe. I didn't think we'd be "reverting back to how we were." We were so weak back then, could die so easily. Now that we couldn't, we knew so much more about the universe. It helped the human race so much, why would we go back to how it was before? So I guess I thought it was a glitch in the system, a stupid glitch but a glitch. But glitches happened every so often to everything right? So wouldn't there be another person with a glitch? Or at least someone else who had a glitch but died or got it fixed? I just didn't know what to think about it.

I sighed and grabbed my phone before sneaking out the window in my room. I slid down the roof and landed on the ground in a crouched position. I'd been practicing that since I was younger, and now it had come in handy. I started walking toward the old school building about a mile east.

I arrived and walked into an old classroom. There was already a man sitting on top of the teacher's desk, waiting for me, most likely.

"Hey," I stated, walking up to him.

"Hello, Andre," the man replied.

"What about your name?" I asked, and put my hand out for him.

"Luke," he stated, taking my hand and shaking it. I wasn't sure how he knew my name, but I figured he wasn't going to hurt me. This had been planned, after all.

"Well, Luke, it's a pleasure," I said and took a step back.

"What are your ideas?" Luke questioned, standing up.

"I want them to know how I feel," I replied. Luke nodded and pulled a piece of paper from his pocket, handing it to me.

"Does this work?" he asked. I looked at the paper, calculating the formula in my head quickly before I looked back up at him.

"Yeah, it works. Can you do it?" I asked and handed him back the paper.

"Yes," he replied. "I'll keep in contact," he continued and then turned, walking from the room.

A few days later, I was lying on my bed reading a book when Luke called me.

"Did you want to do it?" he asked.

"Yes," I said and hung up the phone, going downstairs.

"Bye, Mom!" I called.

"Have fun!" my mom replied, probably thinking I was going to the movies or to lunch or something.

I walked to the factory where Luke worked. He probably lived there but I wasn't at liberty to ask.

There were several men working who looked up when I

walked in. I ignored them and found Luke, who was talking to one of the workers.

"Luke, sir," I stated.

"Andre, come here," he said and motioned for me to follow him. I did and we walked into another room on the side.

"How do you want to do this?" he asked.

"The water supply, that way it would hit everyone," I replied.

"That's what I figured you were going to say. I already have it all set up right over here," he stated and motioned over to a water tank. I walked over to it.

"Will it work?" I asked, turning back to him.

"Yeah, all you have to do is pull the lever, everything else is done," Luke stated.

"Alright," I said and turned back around, putting my hand on the lever.

"People are going to die, you know," Luke said.

"I know," I replied and pulled the lever. I couldn't see what was happening so I just had to trust Luke that it worked.

"Did it work?" I asked.

"Of course," he replied. Now all I had to do was wait. I hoped Luke was right and that it had worked.

Back at home, I was just waiting for some sign that it had worked. My mom hadn't done anything yet so I had no idea. Just then the phone started ringing.

"Hey," I said, answering the phone.

"Hey, Andre, you wanna go down to the lake?" my friend asked.

"Sure, why not?" I replied and hung up. The only reason I ever got invited to the lake was to watch their stuff on the boat. That would change soon.

"Mom, I'm going to the lake!" I yelled, going downstairs and out the door. She didn't reply, probably doing work or something.

I met up with my friends, Max, Sophie, and Jacob, at the edge of the lake. They already had the boat set up, just needed to push it into the water.

"Hey, guys!" I said and jumped into the boat.

"Hey, A!" Jacob said and hopped in with me, looking at the others with a smirk. They had to push the boat in this time.

"You guys have your clones?" I asked Jacob.

"Of course, we always do," he said with a laugh. It was a stupid question. I knew that. He knew it was stupid too. For a second I worried that he knew something, but he didn't. Max and Sophie waded out into the water and jumped into the boat.

"Look what you've done. I'm all wet," Sophie scoffed.

"You were going to end up getting wet anyway. We're at a lake," Jacob laughed.

"I don't need you in my life anymore," she stated with a smile.

"Aw, come on you know you love me!" Jacob fake-pouted and made a move toward her. She smirked and took a step back.

"Catch me if you can," she said and turned, diving off the edge of the boat.

"You were just complaining about being wet!" Jacob yelled at her once she surfaced again. She shrugged and swam toward the boat a little, eyeing Jacob.

"Are you a chicken? You can't come catch me," she stated. Jacob tossed his shirt at me.

"Watch that, choke Max if you need to," he told me.

"Hey!" Max yelled after him, but Jacob had already jumped off the boat. I turned to Max.

"They're idiots," he said shaking his head, and walked over to the steering wheel of the boat. They were playing tag in the water still.

"I hope you guys can swim well enough to keep up with the boat!" Max yelled at them and started driving.

We drove out to the middle of the lake. The bottomless lake, this was the part that seemed bottomless. None of us had actually reached the bottom, it was a couple hundred feet deep. Of course we actually knew there was a bottom. Scientists had figured that out. It was just a challenge to see who could actually get down there first. No one was actually smart enough to bring oxygen tanks. They just swam down until they drowned and then the next person would try. I seriously don't know how these people aged, well, I mean I did. We didn't care what body they were in, they still were that age. On business applications and birth certificates and stuff like that. So I guess they all looked young for their age.

"Andre, you good?" Max asked, cutting me from my thoughts.

"Yeah," I stated and stood up. Jacob and Sophie were having a race toward the boat.

"Whoever wins gets to go down first," Max smiled and walked over to the edge of the boat. I followed him and watched the two race.

Jacob won, he climbed up onto the boat, taunting Sophie about it, who was trying to scowl. She couldn't keep the face though and was laughing.

"You get to go," Max said with a laugh, going to push Jacob overboard.

"Lemme catch my breath," Jacob said, grabbing Max's arm and throwing him overboard. He came above water a few seconds later.

"Eight to nine," he stated, climbing back up on the boat. The two of them had a competition on how many times they could get the other overboard. I don't know how they managed to remember but they had. Usually it ended with both of them going overboard and that would be a tie, which was why the score wasn't really high.

"I'm winning," Jacob smirked.

"Whatever. You go under. Let's see if you really can win," Max said.

"Fine, I'm going," Jacob stated and turned, diving off the boat. He didn't resurface and we knew he wasn't going to. We walked down to the underside part of the boat. Jacob's body was there, sitting in one of the chairs. It was lifeless, the eyes were glazed over and the muscles unmoving. Max and Sophie looked the same. It creeped me out every time I saw a clone, not anyone else. Probably because they had them and I didn't. I'd gotten used to them and could hide the feeling seeing the clones gave me. I looked away and at Max and Sophie. They were arguing about how far down Jacob would go. I sighed and sat down on one of the chairs.

I must've zoned out because I snapped back to attention when Jacob sat up, gasping. He looked around confused for several moments before finally saying, "I almost got there," his senses seeming to come back to him slowly as he got a hold of his surroundings. I tried not to hide my disappointment. What I'd done hadn't worked. Oh well, there would be other chances.

"You did not!" Max yelled.

"Go find out," Jacob smirked and stood up.

"I'll go next!" Sophie yelped and ran up the stairs. We heard a splash and she was gone.

"Give me some water, man," Jacob said after Sophie left, and motioned to a bottle.

"That's Sophie's, you sure?" Max said, walking over and grabbing the half-empty bottle.

"Yeah, I haven't had anything all day and drowning usually makes you thirsty," he replied. Max laughed and tossed the bottle at him.

"Yo, A, you take that into consideration. Whenever you get a gene transplant or however the crap they are going to fix you, always take extra water if you plan on dying. You get thirsty," Jacob said, taking a drink and then throwing the rest at me. I shook out my arms, glaring at him.

"Thanks, I'll consider it. But I might as well bring water to dump on you," I stated. Max and Jacob started talking about school and stuff after that. I said something every now and then but it was mostly them.

About ten minutes later Max turned to Jacob. "Man, I think Sophie beat you," he said.

"IDK, man she's been under for a pretty long time. You think she cheated?" Jacob asked.

"She wouldn't. I'll go look for her," Max replied and turned, going up the stairs. I tried to look like I was worried. But maybe it had worked. This was my only way of knowing. Max came back down a few minutes later.

"I don't see her, shouldn't she have resurfaced by now?" Max asked. He was becoming panicked. That I could tell. Sophie was his sister.

"Should we just turn around and she'll show up?" I suggested. Jacob gave a small nod and headed upstairs. Max gave a look at Sophie's clone before sighing and following Jacob upstairs. I went after them.

Jacob was driving back this time, Max was standing and looking over the edge. I walked over to him and looked out across the water. I didn't see anyone or any movement.

"You good?" I asked.

"She'll turn up, right?" he asked, turning to me, concern written all over his face.

"Yes, she'll turn up," I replied. I wasn't lying. I had just left out the part about her maybe not turning up alive.

"Okay," he nodded and turned back to face the water. I turned and looked back at it too. Still no movement.

It had been days, more incidents like that had been happening since then. The town officials had found Sophie's body. She had drowned, no one could figure out why the gene didn't work and it was scaring people, putting them all on edge. I wasn't going to tell anyone I knew the reason behind it. Today was Sophie's funeral. Max and his family had gotten a lot of crap, a lot of people thought that Sophie had somehow cursed the town. We were on our way to the funeral now.

There weren't very many people there, despite the whole town knowing about her death. I stood near Max and Jacob. A couple of their other friends were there but they didn't like me all too much so no one was talking to me. I'm surprised I was actually even invited to the funeral, it was probably just because I had been there when she passed.

My mother was talking with Max's parents, they had grown up together so that's the only reason Max and I were friends. I saw Luke, why was he there? Yeah, he was part of this town, but he didn't need to be here. Most of the town hadn't come. I walked over to him. He looked up when I walked over.

"What are you doing here?" I asked.

"What you did worked, but you killed an innocent person," he stated.

"She killed herself," I replied.

"You can think that, but now that you've done it what do you plan to do?"

"Nothing. They are scared and they are weak. That's what I wanted," I stated.

"What about when the officials figure out the problem and fix it? They are going to try and find who did it. And guess who is going to be the number one suspect?" Luke said and turned, walking away. I watched him walk away before turning around and walking back to the others.

After the funeral my mom went home with Max. I went back to my house, Jacob and the others went back to his place.

I was watching TV when there was a knock at the door. I sighed and got up to go get it. Sophie's dad was standing there.

"Hello," I said a little uneasily. Why wasn't he with my mom?

"Hello, Andre, may I come in?" he asked.

"Sure," I nodded and opened the door wider, stepping to the side so he could walk in.

"Do you need something?" I asked, closing the door and following after him.

"I just wanted to talk to you," he stated.

"About what?"

"Sophie," he said and turned around. I took a step back, confused.

"What about her?"

"Well, Luke, my boss, came by to offer his condolences and also to tell me that my baby girl was murdered," he stated and took a step forward.

"Murdered? How? She drowned in the lake," I stated blankly, watching him.

"Yeah, no one just drowns. You die of old age. That's all," he replied.

"I really don't know. She jumped off the boat like normal and she never came back up. She might've done something to the clones and killed herself. It's possible, people have done it before," I said.

"The thing is, the officials looked at the clones. There was nothing wrong with them. She, for some reason, didn't go back to them. And the only reason I can think that would cause that is if her gene wasn't working," he stated.

"I really don't know what you want from me, sir," I said, backing up a few steps.

"The only person who has the intelligence and the will to take away someone's gene would be you. What I don't understand is why take it from her and not some random stranger?" he said, advancing on me.

"I wouldn't do something like that to her," I stated.

"Who else would want to remove the gene?" he stated.

"Who said it was removed?" I replied.

"We'll see how intelligent you are once I tell the town officials what you did," he snapped and pushed past me back to the door.

"They can't do anything if there's no evidence," I stated, turning to face him.

"There will be evidence. And you think anyone will listen to your side of the story? You're an abomination," he practically snarled before turning and walking out, the door slamming behind him.

I sighed and walked back into the living room, collapsing on the couch. He was right, the officials wouldn't listen to me, evidence or not. But would they take his story without evidence? That, I didn't know.

My mother walked in a few minutes later, she walked toward me with concern written on her face.

"I'm fine," I stated, standing up.

"Everyone thinks you had something to do with it. Do you?" she asked, looking at me like I was a different person.

"No. I can't murder someone. How could you think that?" I questioned.

"I believe you, but tell *them*," she stated and stepped aside. One of the officials had walked in, his jacket pulled to the side so I could see the badge. It's not like I needed to, you could tell an official from a mile away.

"You can't do anything. There's no evidence that shows I killed anyone. You're just going to take another man's word? He's in grief. He'll blame anyone for her death," I stated and took a step forward, my eyes on the official.

"We'll see," the official stated before continuing. "We can't do anything to you yet, even though I'd like to, we can just bring you in for questioning. Are you willing to?" the official asked. If I said no I'd be going unwillingly so there wasn't really any question in his sentence.

"I'll go," I sighed and walked past him to the car. He said something to my mom quickly before following me out.

We were in the questioning room. I wasn't an idiot, they were totally faking it, just looking for some evidence to put me behind bars. There was a one-way mirror in the room. It was pretty obvious and the official had a gun and handcuffs on him, both of which were illegal to have when you were just bringing someone in for questioning. This wasn't even a questioning room, it was an execution room that had been cleaned. I wasn't sure if this was supposed to scare me or if they just thought I was really stupid. I was sitting down and the official was standing up, his hand constantly going to his waist, where the gun was. Did he think I was going to attack him? What could I do?

"You were on the lake when she drowned. Correct?" he asked.

"Yes. With Max and Jacob," I stated.

"What happened?" The official took a step toward me, his hand still on his waist. I did my best to ignore it and looked at him.

"We were in the underside of the boat. Jacob had just woken up and claimed he could see the bottom. Sophie wanted to beat him so she ran upstairs. We heard her jump in the water and she never resurfaced," I replied.

"Well, you never expected her to resurface," he stated.

"No, we didn't. It was a game we played. We expected her to clone but she never did," I said.

"Why is that?" he asked.

"I don't know. I know as much as everyone else," I snapped and started to stand up. He shot me a glare and I sat back down uneasily.

"People only stop cloning once the gene is overused and dies," the official said, talking as if I didn't already know.

"Well, maybe it's something genetic and it died off faster," I said.

"What about the others of the town? What happened to them?" the official asked.

"I do not know," I stated. The official sighed and turned, leaving the room. I knew he was talking to someone on the other side of the door.

He came back a few minutes later with a smirk on his face. He walked over till he was just a couple of inches away from my face.

"Sir, did you need something?" I questioned and leaned back in my chair as much as was physically possible without moving the chair.

"Explain this," he said and pulled out a piece of paper, shoving it in my face.

"It's a paper, sir," I stated and looked up at him, confused.

"What's on it?" he snapped and brought it back so I could see the words.

"A formula," I replied.

"What's the formula do?" he snarled.

"How should I know? I didn't make it."

"You're the smartest kid in the town and you don't know what that is?" he questioned, on the verge of losing whatever calm was left.

"Yeah, I suppose so," I said slowly, unsure of how he wanted the question to be answered.

"It's evidence against you is what it is," he snapped and turned, walking from the room again.

He came back about thirty minutes later, he said something to another man in the doorway. The other man never came in, just nodded and closed the door. The official walked in, less angry than before.

"You are under arrest," he stated.

"Why?" I asked, starting to stand up.

"For the murder of Sophie White and the destruction of the cloning gene in this town," he said and took a step forward.

"I-I don't know what you're talking about," I said and backed up, putting the chair between the two of us.

"Luke said you forced him to use his workers to make that formula and put it in the water supply."

"I didn't do that! He did that willingly!" I yelled, backing up more.

"I don't believe you for a second, and your DNA is all over that paper. So you know that the formula could have temporarily shut down the genes," the official said, his hand going to his waist. I followed his hand, my eyes glued to the weapon.

"That doesn't mean I ever used the formula!" I said, pushing myself, panicked, against the wall.

"It explains what happened to the town. It leaves you responsible for five deaths," the official said calmly, raising his gun.

"Please don't shoot," I stated, my voice ten times quieter than it had just been.

"I'm sorry, but the five people who died are telling me I should," the official said with a smirk and pulled the trigger.

I reacted too late and the bullet found home in my head. My body slumped forward, no longer focused on standing up but more on the injury. Everything was blurry and swimming in and out of focus. I saw the official come toward me, the smirk still on his face. I struggled to stand up and ignore the tunnel vision I had gained. This made the pain in my head worse. I fell back down with a cry. I saw the official's mouth move as if he said something but I didn't hear him. He raised his gun again and then, blackness.

Silent Words

MY MOTHER DRANK stories with her morning coffee, a warm broth of words mixed with the paragraphs, the commas, and the periods. They came in various flavors. Some were sweet, others bitter, but they were all appetizing when she read to my sister and me. We devoured the stories whole. The words poured out of her like a waterfall. Every day I'd run home from school, tremendously thirsty, and would drink from the abundance of stories she provided. Our family was dizzy with the love for words.

I wondered how she did it. She had the power to lift emotions from the pages and implant them into the hearts of the audience. How had my mother mastered this art? If she told me that she was a magician, I may have believed her. Every story she read cast a spell on me.

Why was it that I had not inherited her magical ability? Whenever I attempted to read aloud, it was as if sand were crawling through my throat. I tried to read until I thought I would cough up blood if I tried anymore. Still, no words ever dared to climb out.

Most people assumed shyness was the cause of my silence. Concerned teachers often emailed my mother, asking why I never spoke in class. It was embarrassing, but my mother was never upset with me. She embraced the fact that I was different from others. My sister, on the other hand, wasn't very fond of me. She forbid me from being near her outside of the house, worried that I would try to speak and have people laugh at us. It had happened before.

The bell rang one afternoon, signaling the end of the school day. I was about to run home when I heard someone call my name. "Hey, Miriam! Come over here!"

I turned around and recognized some of my classmates huddled together. They waved. I hesitated, not knowing why they were calling me.

"Hello? What are you waiting for? Come on," they yelled.

I trudged toward them, feeling skeptical. Despite my attempt to keep my distance, they threw their arms over my shoulders and dragged me in closer. My heartbeat loudly protested in my chest.

"So, Miriam, you've been awfully quiet the entire school year. Why don't you talk to us a bit, huh?" someone said with a hint of sarcasm. I didn't answer.

"Aw, come on. Don't be shy." Another classmate roughly grabbed my arm and tried to pull me in closer. Startled, I tried to scream "Stop!" but instead a hideous croak came out. They erupted in laughter.

"What was that?" they asked, cackling. Ashamed, I tried to pull away. They wouldn't let me go.

Suddenly I noticed my sister, Maria, a few feet away from me. Her eyes were wide open with shock. Relief washed over me when she began to walk toward us.

"Hey," one of them asked her, "do you know this girl?"

Maria remained quiet, a look of hesitation wandered through her eyes. The words that escaped her lips hurt more than the unknown hands digging through my shoulders. "No," she whispered, "I don't know her."

She watched as they continued to laugh and shove me. I gave her a menacing glare. She seemed like she wanted to say she was sorry, but her desire to be loved by her peers prevented her from doing so.

When they let me go, I ran home crying. Maria chased after me, screaming, "I'm sorry, Miriam! I'm sorry!" Forgiveness was unimaginable.

My mother was furious when she found out. I heard her pacing back and forth in the room next to mine all night. I hated myself for causing her distress. All I wanted was to make her proud, but all I gave her was worry. I despised myself for being such a terrible daughter.

The next morning, my mother announced that I wouldn't be attending that school anymore. Maria walked to school by herself, as she always did, leaving my mother and me alone together. *Why, Mom?* I signed, letting my fingers speak for me.

"I think this new school would be better for you, Miriam. I've heard a lot of nice things about it, and they have more resources that could help you," she replied.

They're all the same. No matter how many times I switch schools, people will treat me like an outsider.

"That's not true, Miriam. There are many kind and understanding people in the world."

Where are they? Even my own sister won't help me when I am in need! Tears trickled down my face. My mother hugged me.

"I'm here for you," she said. "Just try this new school, okay? If it doesn't work out, we can try something else."

My mother drove me to my new school the following day. It was a bit farther away, but I enjoyed the early-morning scenery that nature displayed through the car window. The tall trees were glowing under the radiant sun, and the birds flew by us gracefully. I felt calm until the car paused in front of a voluminous white building. Dozens of students were wandering around. My mother clasped my hand and gave it a light squeeze.

"Be strong, Miriam. Text me if you need anything," she offered.

I nodded and climbed out of the car. I took a deep breath and waved goodbye to my mother, pretending I couldn't see the tears in her eyes.

The halls were slightly less crowded than the ones at my previous school, but they were overflowing with sound. It was easy to disappear in the loud conversations and gossip.

"Are you the new student?" A woman suddenly appeared, causing me to jump.

"Sorry, I didn't mean to startle you," she apologized. "I'm Ms. Park, the English teacher. Nice to meet you. Miriam, right?"

I nodded, pretending that I was distracted by the posters on the walls.

"Are you interested in our writing contest?" she asked.

I looked up, noticing the huge black-and-white words scrawled on one of the posters.

"All students can submit a story. It can be anything you'd like.

You should try it! Just submit it to me before the end of next week," Ms. Park explained.

The thought of entering intrigued me. It was my chance to speak my mind without actually speaking.

"Let me know if you have any questions, okay?" She smiled as she walked away.

The school day ended quickly. No one forced me to talk, and I was able to respond to the questions I received by nodding my head. I prayed that I could be silent for the rest of the school year without seeming suspicious, but I knew that wouldn't be the case.

My mother drove me home. The ride was silent until we reached a red light.

She looked at me nervously. "How was school, Miriam?"

It was fine.

She smiled. "I'm so glad. What did you do today? Any news?"

I might enter a writing contest.

Her smile expanded, lighting up her entire face. "Really? That's great! You should definitely do it!"

The light turned green, and the silence resumed once again. I contemplated what I would write about. There were many stories growing in my head. I was eager to nurture them until they bloomed.

At home, I sat by my desk with a blank sheet of paper in front of me. I closed my eyes and searched for the stories hidden within me. My mother's delicate voice crept through my mind. Her stories were like honey, so scrumptious that anyone who listened begged for more. I searched my mind for a story as sweet as honey, and let it flow through my pen and drip onto the paper. My mother always told me that satisfying stories came from the heart.

Then, suddenly, I had it. What story could be closer to my heart than my own?

After a week of intense writing, I had my heart written on paper. I handed it to Ms. Park with a huge smile on my face.

"Is this your entry for the writing contest?" Ms. Park asked. I nodded.

She grinned. "Great. I'll give this back to you at the awards ceremony tomorrow. It will be in the yard after school. Will you be there?" I nodded again.

"Awesome. See you then!"

I daydreamed about the contest the entire day. My mother noticed my exhilaration when she picked me up from school.

"What are you so excited about?"

I entered the writing contest.

"That's fantastic! When will the results be revealed?"

There will be an awards ceremony tomorrow after school.

"Can I come?"

Sure.

"How about Maria?"

I paused. The laughter of the bullies replayed in my head.

"Miriam?"

I don't think she wants to come.

"Why not?"

I'll only embarrass her.

"Honey, that's not true."

It's true, Mom.

"Nonsense. She will be there." There was no point in arguing with her. My mother was a woman of words.

On the day of the ceremony, crowds of students gathered in front of a stage. I struggled to find Ms. Park.

"Miriam!" someone yelled.

I turned around and saw Ms. Park running toward me.

"There you are. Here is your story." She handed it to me. "You'll be reading it aloud in ten minutes. Get on the stage. Good luck!" She left before I could protest.

My voice betrayed me once again. How was I supposed to tell her that I couldn't read aloud?

I analyzed the crowd. Everyone was expecting me to appear onstage. My mother was standing next to Maria. She waved at me.

"Students, if you are participating in the contest, please get onstage now," Ms. Park announced. I had no choice.

My body shook as the students read their stories one by one. I envied their beautiful voices. The more time passed, the tighter the hands of fear clutched my heart and lungs. I contemplated how I could escape this situation. Maybe I could pretend I was sick or . . .

"Miriam, it's your turn." Too late.

I stumbled to the microphone. A myriad of eyes stared at me, expecting me to use the voice I did not have. I closed my eyes and took a deep breath, placing my paper on the floor in front of me. I lifted my hands. There was only one thing I could do.

My mother drank stories with her morning coffee, I explained using sign language. The crowd began to whisper, but I continued.

A warm broth of words mixed with the paragraphs, the commas, and the periods.

"My mother drank stories with her morning coffee, a warm broth of words mixed with the paragraphs, the commas, and the periods." I looked down and saw Ms. Park with the crowd. She was speaking into the microphone.

Go on, she signed.

They came in various flavors. Some were sweet, others bitter, but they were all appetizing when she read to my sister and me.

"They came in various flavors. Some were sweet, others bitter, but they were all appetizing when she read to my sister and me." Ms. Park smiled.

When I finished the story, everyone cheered. My mother brushed the tears away from her face as my sister screamed, "That's my sister! That's my sister!"

I exited the stage. Ms. Park was waiting there for me. She enveloped me in her arms.

How do you know sign language? I asked.

I'm deaf, Ms. Park responded, leaving me astonished.

Why didn't you tell me sooner?

Ms. Park let out a tiny laugh. She put her hand on my shoulder.

How else could I teach you to believe in yourself?

She handed me a certificate for first place. *Have you learned your lesson, Miriam?*

I nodded. *Yes.*

CARLO   DI   BERNARDO

The Sickle

As I TURNED the corner, facing into Carlo's bedroom, the first thing I saw was the untidy empty bed. I sensed something was wrong, because he was out of his bed so early, and immediately I noticed the glimmer of dark red on the sheets. Stepping in, past the covers on the floor, I peered over his pillow, completely soaked in blood with plucked-out feathers. My mind raced, heart sank, and I froze. When I found him he was in the bathroom, looking at his face in horror and shock, as the entire right side was drenched in burgundy dried blood.

"I was out with friends last night but I came home around eleven fifteen and everything was normal. I went to bed around midnight, if I remember correctly," Carlo told me in an agitated manner. My thoughts went back to last night, remembering that I had come home at around 1:00 a.m. His door was closed, lights were off, and the house was dead silent. Had it already happened by then? What happened in his room from twelve to one? *What the hell happened?!* On Monday, at school, everyone asked Carlo this same question upon looking at his swollen and stitched face. Truth is, everyone in the family, including Carlo, was mulling over the same thing. He later confessed to me that every time someone asked that question he felt his stomach turn, knowing that all he could say was, "I don't know."

Saturday afternoon, in the surgeon's office, Carlo's face was cleaned up of all the blood. A couple of hours before, Carlo had told me, "Okay, it's a little weird but everyone is actually overre-acting . . . it's just a cut, I probably just rubbed against the windowsill while sleeping." So he thought, but what he referred to as a cut started dead center between his eyes, right above his nose, reaping its way down to the bottom of his right cheek. "One centimeter deep," the surgeon told him as he pulled away from his forehead. "That's not rubbing against something. Whatever it was, it made it all the way to your skull," he said minutes before Carlo was given twenty-one stitches. I remember Carlo's trembling body when he was told that the cut would be visible on his face forever—all I was thinking was how the cut resembled the exact shape of a sickle. Not only that, what struck me the most was that the shape of the cut followed the flow of a hand motion . . . This was no accident.

On Friday, the day it happened, Carlo had neglected all the spooky correlations and myths regarding that day. He had never conceived to be scared by such seemingly foolish superstitions. Because it hadn't been just any Friday. "Carlo, it was midnight . . . on Friday the 13th," Joey told Carlo to explain the ominous mystery.

Carlo told his dad on Sunday night, "I slept perfectly, not waking up once between midnight and seven thirty. The first time I felt any pain was when I was given stitches." On Saturday morning, I looked around his room, but there was virtually nothing sharp enough to make such an incision. "The last time I dealt with a scar so deep was when my patient got stabbed by one of their family members with a kitchen knife." From the surgeon's seemingly relaxed voice, I presumed this incident was accidental. The sharpest object I found in Carlo's room was a bluntly sharpened Ticonderoga pencil. I snooped around more and discovered that although his balcony door was closed, it was unusually unlocked. Nevertheless, nothing on his balcony was sharp enough to cut him and we know for sure he did not jump off the balcony. "Maybe someone came in from outside," speculated another of Carlo's classmates, and that did seem viable. At first it seemed absurd to Carlo, but the more he thought of it the more probable it felt. If the cut was so deep, someone must have done it to him . . . but who? and why?

In the meantime, Carlo was going to all sorts of specialists, yet not one was able to explain what could have happened that night. One week after the incident, Carlo was growing increasingly annoyed. "I don't want to talk about this anymore, the more we discuss it the stranger it feels," he would tell us. Mom kept insisting that he was a somnambulist, someone who walks in his sleep. She maintains that Carlo left home in the middle of the night, something happened to his face, and he came back to his bed, all in his sleep.

The whole household, including Carlo, said they slept like angels. That shows everyone is as likely to be a sleepwalker as Carlo. I even wondered whether I could be capable of such profanation in my sleep. What's weirdest of all is that the only place where blood was found in the entire house was in Carlo's bed. Therefore, whatever happened, happened in his bed? "It's almost as if every possible solution contradicts the facts and what we know," one of the many specialists said. Unless witnesses were lying regarding what they did that night, this statement is most utterly accurate. Say he is a sleepwalker, then who did it to him? Why would anyone attack him? Did he do it to himself? If he did, could it have been in his room? With what? In his house? Why was there blood nowhere else but in his bed? How did Carlo not feel any pain, wake up, or remember it? These unsolved questions are why the case remains enshrouded in mystery.

Last week, on Friday, Carlo slept on the floor of my room. I was too tired to ask him why he didn't just sleep in his own room, but as soon as I closed my eyes the words *Friday the 13th* glimmered in the dark, followed by a bloody sickle.

KYLA DUHART

The Unfortunate Tale
of Sam Withersby

DEAR KATE,

I am writing to you because I know you are the only one who will understand. You are the only person who would believe me. You know me better than anyone else and would never for a second believe I would do such a horrible thing without just reason. So here goes nothing . . . This is the real story of how my mom and father died.

It all started five years ago when my mother finally called the police and reported my father. My mother feared him and was terrified of the consequences that came with turning him in to the police for beating her, but I was glad she did because I couldn't have taken one more night of watching him throw or punch her each and every time she didn't do everything he asked then and there. She spent hours in the mirror trying to cover up every scar, bruise, and pain that she felt inside and out. This was my life for about nine years until September 30, 2011, when Mr. Lock, one of San Diego Police Department's finest, put the metal handcuffs around my father and took him away.

My mom was smart, she didn't wait around for him to be set free. She made us pack up our stuff, hop on a plane, and move to the house next door to yours. I loved being in that house. I never had to worry about my mother making the wrong move or getting thrown and punched because she didn't make a sandwich exactly as he wanted. That house was a gateway to happiness. I would get home from school sometimes and my mother would be there waiting with a giant smile on her face because she knew that we were finally safe. My mom got a job as a business assistant—nothing special, but it did pay the bills and her hours worked beautifully into our lives, which made us happy and we hadn't had that feeling in a long time.

I apologize to you, Kate, for never telling you. You're my best friend, but I couldn't even think of my father without breaking into tears, and frankly I did not want to talk about him. I was ashamed that my only father would be nothing more than a coward. So I pretended that I didn't have a father at all.

Anyway, you remember that day when I went home early and the next day you asked me why I was being so distant? Well, I went home early that day because my mother got a phone call from a friend back in San Diego telling her that my father served his sentence and was free. She also informed my mother that he came to their house asking where we were. He was back and he was going to find us one way or another, it was only a matter of time. My mom couldn't stop crying that day and became overprotective. She would get up at all hours of the night to make sure that the windows were closed, the doors were locked, and that I was still safely sleeping in my bedroom. She even put a tracker in my phone so she'd know where I was at all times, but I'd rather have gone through all those precautions than wake up one morning and find him in our house.

Later, I came to realize that some nightmares are meant to come true, we just weren't aware of how soon.

Well, I guess I should elaborate on that since you haven't seen me in about a week. The last day I saw you was the day I came home from school and saw my father sitting on my porch with a gun on his lap and black leather gloves on. He made me open the door and we walked inside. He gave a lecture on how we shouldn't have left, betrayed his love, or even tried to escape, because he was always going to be around. He made it seem as if living with him was like being locked away without any hope of ever getting away, and with all honesty it was. I don't know what was going on in my head at the time, but all I could think about was making him disappear because that speech made every pain he caused us to come back and wound me all over again.

"Do you want any water?" I asked, wondering if he would actually let me get away, even for a second, so I could clear my head. To my surprise he nodded yes. So I got up, walked into the kitchen, turned on the faucet, grabbed a cup, filled it with water, and snatched a knife from the bottom drawer and shoved it in my pocket.

"Hurry up in there, I am thirsty here. Oh! And put some ice in there, if you have any, it's not like you guys can afford much. Your mother can't do anything right, so I doubt she has a good-paying job. Or any job, for that matter."

I hated him. How dare he make the assumption that my mother can't do anything? But I knew it was best for me not to say any of this because who knows what he would've done with that gun.

"We don't have any ice, but our faucet water gets really cold if you run it for a little while," I said with irritation as I realized who I was serving. I couldn't believe he had found us. My mom had tried too hard to close the past and focus on our future for it all to be shattered now. I walked back into the living room, handed him his water. We watched each other intently, waiting to see what would happen next, but the adrenaline was eating me alive. I needed to get away, so I pulled out the knife and sliced his shin and made a run for my bike outside, but it was too late. By the time I unlocked the chain his gun was held at the back of my head.

"Get inside now!!" He was angry. The type of anger that he had when he nearly beat my mother to death. We walked inside slowly. I was trembling with fear and dropped the knife, so all I could do was wonder if anyone would save me from this monster, but unfortunately people don't always get help when they need it most.

"Get out a piece of paper and pen," he demanded. I didn't have any other choice than to listen to what I was told. So I went inside my backpack, pulled out a notebook and a pen.

"I want you to write exactly what I tell you!! Nothing more or less. Got it?" I nodded my head in fear so he would stop inching closer and closer with the gun. This was the first time in my life where I felt true fear and couldn't do a thing about it.

Once I was done writing the note I taped it to the front door and we walked to his car. Now, you'd figure this guy would have the decency to let me ride in the "car," but no, I was shoved in the trunk for who knows how long to who knows where. Sounds fun, right?

Anyways, when the car came to an official halt, he opened the trunk and walked me inside an abandoned warehouse, where I was tied to a pole and teased with the thought of food, but all I could really think about was my mother. How she felt when she was getting home, expecting to see her daughter after a long day of work, to find a note that read:

He's back.

That was it. How could she know where to look, go, or even know who "he" was? It would have been practically impossible for her to find me, or so I thought. And I also couldn't understand the thought of how my own father would do this to me. I was his only child, his own blood, and here I sat hungry, tied to a pole, and forced to listen to his complaints and laughter about what he had to go through in Watson's County Jail and how my mother wouldn't live to regret the day she dialed 911.

That day couldn't have gotten any worse, or so I believed, until about midnight when I heard a car pull up and somebody tiptoeing toward the warehouse.

"Sam. Sammy are you here? Your phone tracked you here. Are you here?"

"Mom!! I'm in here. Please come. Help me!" I yelled, oblivious to the fact that I had woken my father.

My mom ran in with a knife, the same one I had dropped on the floor back at the house, and proceeded to cut the ropes that bound me to the pole. She then pointed the knife at my father.

"How dare you? How dare you take my baby? She did nothing wrong!! This is between you and me. I have let you take away so much from me, you are not getting anything more!!" she screamed as she lunged toward him with the knife. I needed to help her, but I was so weak. What could I do? *The gun!!* I remembered. I ran to where my father was sitting and grabbed the gun, but it was too late. My mother was dead on the floor. He'd stabbed her. How could he have stabbed her?! I panicked and I was flustered with anger. So I picked up the gun, held it firm in my hands, and pulled the trigger without any remorse.

I called the police and reported the incident and they arrested me. Me!! He deserved to die, but the facts were these: my fingerprints were on both weapons, I admitted to killing my father, my father wore gloves, not a single drop of blood of my mother's was on him, and I was only fourteen with two murdered parents beside me. So I was pegged as mental and sent to the Maulsby Asylum. Where I get to sit every day in a white room with soft pillows and write about my feelings and to you.

I'm sorry to end us this way, but if you haven't learned from before, not everyone gets their happy ending, and frankly it's not always deserved. So this is goodbye, Kate.

Sincerely,
Sam Withersby

Dream World

I REMEMBER WAKING UP. It felt as if I had been submerged in the dark for eons, finally coming up for a breath of luminescence. Tiny amoebas played in my field of vision as my eyes adjusted to the world outside the Cimmerian shade I had escaped from. The curtains next to me were drawn back to reveal a soft pink whisper of morning. My eyes fixated upon a bright red hot air balloon painted on a cerulean tile; a fragment of a glistening mosaic that reflected the blossoming morning sun as flickers of color and light engaged in a vivacious tango, causing the plain walls around me to erupt into a moving, breathing kaleidoscope.

I was so mesmerized by the light show that the creaking of a door swinging open startled me out of my daze.

"Beautiful morning, isn't it? I'm glad to see you awake." A woman with a luscious head of hair that would fit right in to a Pantene commercial stood at the door, eyes sweeping over me in a brisk inspection.

I opened my mouth to speak but was overwhelmed by the dryness that seemed to have set up camp in my throat. I could barely produce a croak.

The woman cleared her throat and tapped her long, well-manicured nails against her clipboard.

"I am Dr. Em. You must be wondering quite a lot of things. I'm here to help you along the journey to recovery and answer any questions you may have."

Despite her gracious offer, I noticed an authoritative note in her voice, mixed with the deep indent of a smile line dimpling her left cheek.

Slowly, her words sank in and I felt as if I had been struck with a hot coal iron.

"Recovery?' I asked.

I glanced around the room once more. The dripping IV next to my bed assaulted my vision, and a daunting machine was clear-cut in the dreamy light, producing soft pings in a meticulous cadence. My eyes drifted from the needle seemingly cemented in my vein over to the gown printed with a lackluster vintage rose design that drooped off my shockingly narrow shoulders.

Suddenly I wanted to get out of this bed. I had no recollection of how I had gotten there and had no interest in staying any longer. Weakly, I pushed up on my arms. They seemed to shake with the very effort of holding up my skeletal torso and the pinging of the machine increased its rhythm.

"I wouldn't do that, hon." A concerned Dr. Em watched from the doorway, with one inky well-threaded eyebrow arched.

I leaned my body toward the side of the bed in an attempt to dismount from the cushy mattress, but my legs didn't follow. It felt as if there were an electric current racing through my legs, but I had no control over the movement of my lower limbs. An uneasy feeling gnawed at my gut as I stared at my legs. They seemed to be detached from my body as I took in their condition —thin, dumb, and limp.

I felt like an astronaut who had been launched without instruction. Lost, floating aimlessly in space, encompassed in constellations I could not map and planets I could not recognize. The absence of gravity caused my brain to feel dizzy and I felt as if I was going to crash ungracefully down to Earth at any moment. My mind brimmed with buzzing questions as I tried to focus on Dr. Em, but my vision was clouded with frustrated tears and my front teeth clamped down on my lip so forcibly I could taste the metallic jolt of blood on my tongue.

"W-why can't I move my legs?" I said in the fullest voice I could muster.

Dr. Em finally crossed the threshold and materialized at the foot of my bed.

"Penny, I am going to be direct with you. I believe you are

mature enough to be informed of your condition. By medical definition, you are a paraplegic, meaning you are immobile from the waist down due to a spinal injury from your car accident. You may also be suffering from symptoms of short- or possible long-term amnesia due to the colossal impact you experienced when you crashed."

My thoughts sprinted in a thousand different directions as I sluggishly grasped at what she was saying. A salty taste rose up in the back of my throat as the flavor enveloped my mouth and my stomach convulsed, causing an upside-down geyser to rush out of my mouth into the conveniently located bedpan beside me. Tears began to run freely down my blazing cheeks as I buried my fingers into my knotted hair. I wanted nothing more than to run. For a brief second, I found solace in the fantasy of myself running, running so fast and hard that I encircled the earth once, twice, then three times. The return to reality was crushing. My world was a hula hoop ringing a young child's waist, about to lose its swinging rhythm and collide with the ground in an unsuspecting instant.

I was overcome with exhaustion at the crushing weight of what Dr. Em had told me, throwing my head into my gossamer pillow, the plush material seeming to swallow my face. I squeezed my eyes shut and willed the world to return to the black I now longed to be drenched in, suddenly feeling a comforting warmness as the dark crept in.

A scent of salt water and cinnamon overtook me as crashing waves rumbled and rushed; the tide engaged in a playful wrestling match with the undercurrent. A laugh like a soprano bell tinkled, reverberating on an alkaline breeze. I looked up toward the direction of the musical amusement and saw the glowing face of a woman, seeming to mirror the sun with the warmth of her smile.

"Hey, look who's up!" The woman's toasty chestnut hair whipped around as she gushed down at me. The smell of cinnamon was rich and gave me an inexplicable sense of security.

"My little Penny, come, darling, look what I found." She enthusiastically patted the spot next to her, grains of sand bouncing playfully around her hand.

I somehow found myself standing on tiny sandaled feet and toddled over, sand wedging itself between my toes while the wind blew some onto my chubby legs.

The woman held up an exquisite conch shell, a glaring shade of white decorated with spirals and ridges delicately etched upon its carapace, with a shy salmon lip peeking out.

"Listen, sweetie." She put it to my ear. "The shells know the language of the mermaids, and if you try your very best to hear, it will whisper the secrets of the ocean to you."

Her melodic laugh chimed, and I breathed in cinnamon as the shell whispered sweet nothings to me in the vernacular of the sea.

My surroundings shifted and the sand I was squatting in metamorphosed to dirt-red dust. My once-white sports pants were now a sullied russet in the knee. My hands were dirty with grime as I stood up, dusting myself off and adjusting my burgundy cap.

"Okay, Davidson, you're up to bat next," an abrasive baritone barked at me.

I stood at the heart of the copper field, a diamond panorama of dirt rimmed with grass stretched before me. My gaze migrated to the steel bleachers framing the vicinity, in search of someone. A man waved at me, beaming with a wide boyish smile that peeked out from under his burgundy cap.

My grip on the bat tightened as the pressure of the game and roaring midafternoon heat of the sun impressed upon me, encasing my body in a hot layer of sweat. I allowed myself a deep humid breath as I watched the pitcher begin to wind back her royal-blue-sleeved arm. The next few moments happened just as they would have in a movie; the softball came bludgeoning through the boiling air and made contact with my bat with an echoing *smack!* Letting the bat clunker to the ground, I dashed. My cleats beat against the dirt, rhythmically pounding while my arms swung back and forth, back and forth. It was like I was racing across the sands of Mars while the Martians attempted in an unorganized effort to catch the ball I had sent off into space. I ran and ran, gulping in the fever of the sun. The home base was meters, feet, inches away. I slid home on my knees, hearing a gleeful holler from across the field.

"That's my lucky Penny!" The man in the bleachers was waving manically, breaking into a poorly choreographed victory dance, thrusting his hips forward and back in time with his arms.

I managed a weak smile before the never-ending heat bore down on me and I felt like I was suffocating in a sweltering blanket of sun rays. Black spots dotted my vision and I began spiraling into a nebulous haze.

Awakening this time was different. The shock of the blaring sun's radiance commanded me back into the world of light. The red balloon twinkled at me and I heard the soulful caws of crows serenading the afternoon outside my window.

The door creaked open once more, and a faint smell of cinnamon wafted into the room. The smiling woman from the beach manifests in front of me, her delicate feminine hand tightly clasped into a much larger, stronger one. A boyish smile gleams at me, and the beautiful couple seem to glow in the sunbeams that merengue upon the walls. The room is once more alive, I breathe in time with it as I take in the vision in front of me.

"Mom? Dad?" I say. My voice is barely audible, scratching the surface of a whisper.

Smiling eyes swim with tears as I am swallowed up in a bear hug that hinders my next breath.

"It will be okay, lucky Penny. Everything will be okay."

It was four o'clock.

BETHANY HALL

Noli Me Tangere

SHE TURNS THE KNOB to release hot water for a shower. As she undresses, the memory returns. Guilt embraces her like a loving friend's hug. Maybe it *would* be a friend if she had explained what happened.

She steps into the foggy atmosphere and lets the water burn away her secret. It lingers in the pores of her skin and cracks on her lips. She reaches for the rag and begins to scrub at the secret. It burns. The memory of his hands on her returns, flashing through her mind and touching her skin. Tears like razor blades run down her face. The hot water adds to the burning. She begins to scrub harder.

Her skin turns red and blotchy, but she ignores the signs her body is pleading for her to notice. Scrubbing and scrubbing, she attempts to wash away the feelings he left on her skin and in her memory. Then she remembers that he not only touched her body but also kissed her face and ran his fingers through her hair.

No. No. No!

She pours shampoo in her hand, then reaches up, digging her nails into her skull, trying to get his hands to stop stroking her hair soothingly. Once, twice, three times she pours the shampoo. Once, twice, three times she drags her hands through her hair. The memory of his lips on her face returns to her mind, and it's almost as if it's all happening again. She turns around and stuffs her face under the water.

She reaches for the rag again. She begins to scrub her face. Her acne aches, but it is scrubbed off before the trace of kisses is. She begins wishing she were depressed again. She doesn't want to feel the guilt and pain. Most of all, she doesn't want to feel his memory.

Shh, it's just me. Don't you trust me? She covers her ears and collapses out of the shower. The air is stuffy, her skin burning, her face has strings of blood running down it, but she doesn't notice. She grabs her headphones from the top of her school bag. Quickly, she taps the screen and drags the dot to drown out his pleasant voice.

I'm not going to hurt you . . . His taunting eyes appear in her head. *It's alright . . .* His smile. She tries to focus on the spinning fan and pounding music.

Hey, look at me . . . His deep blue eyes dance on the ceiling.

She squeezes her eyes and covers her face. *Come on . . .* He whispers through his perfect lips.

"No . . ."

You aren't afraid, are you? His hand wraps around hers. His hair too real to just be a memory projecting on the ceiling.

"Don't."

Movement surrounds them.

"Stop."

He turns her, pressing her back against the wall.

"No."

He comes in closer.

"No!"

She kicks and screams, trying to hit him, but his hold on her is too strong.

"Get off!"

She screams, but the music is too loud.

He's getting closer and closer. He pushes her harder and harder.

She feels herself stumble out of her mind as if waking up.

She opens her eyes. The fan is spinning wildly; the lights shake with it. She sits up, expecting to see *him* in front of her again. She tries to focus on details in the room. The white bookshelf, the gray walls, and the black bedsheets . . . the room is empty. What else was there? Where are the friends in front of her, shaking her, telling her it was all just a dream? And if they weren't telling her it was a dream, why weren't they replacing guilt's embrace with theirs? If they said nothing and did nothing, that would've been better than what was actually there. No one.

Only a Fool Would

MY SOFA WAS IN SHREDS, dining ware was scattered all over the floor, and, *wait a minute,* were there holes in my backyard? Wading through the destruction, I reached the screen door to the backyard, which was ripped to shreds, and stared in dumbfoundedness at the eight flawless holes in my grass. They were arranged to form a box-like shape with two holes on each side, as if encasing something in the middle. Stifling an exasperated sigh, I heard a creak. I looked up, not knowing what I would see, but *what the hell?!* A sword hung from my ceiling, with its hilt swinging precariously in the air. Even though it was suspended above me I could see the dent that it created in my ceiling, wedged in between the bright white paint. *Thunk!* It fell to the floor, bringing down pieces of crumbling ceiling as well.

Shrieking, I brought my hands up to cover my hair, my beautiful blond hair, while wondering why everything awful was happening to me. I leaned closer, peering at the instrument. It was dangerous and sharp, as if just looking at it could cut a person right through their eyes. The hilt was weathered and worn, covered with thick leather. Words were etched onto the blade, written in some sort of foreign, ancient language. As I stepped closer, I felt an otherworldly pull, the object itself wanted me to come closer, as if it was an entity. Curiosity overcame my fear, and I leaned over to put my forefinger on the silvery gray blade.

"*Who dares?*" yelled an inanimate voice, filling my destroyed room with sonorous sound.

"*Aagh!*" I yelled, falling on my butt. The thing spoke! "W-Who are you?" I asked, frightened beyond my wits.

What was it doing here? What . . . what was going on? If it was the cause of the destruction in my home, I should call the police, or look for the owner of the threatening weapon. If the police were involved, however, they would find out that I was squatting in this house. The only reason I was never found out was because the house was immaculate on the inside, but demolished on the outside. Therefore, I was determined to find the answers myself; I touched the sword again. This time I pressed my forefinger into the tip of the blade, drawing some blood, which I looked at with fascination. It really was that sharp.

"Tell me who you are," I said with more authority.

"Oh . . . Oh, I apologize, my fair lady, I would never have yelled if I knew you were a woman," it said with an audible smirk in its voice. If it were a person, I could see the smug little smile painted on its face. Nonetheless, I blushed; no one had spoken to me like that before.

"Please, sit, I have a story to tell you."

I frowned, tilting my head to the side, and sunk into the shreds of my sofa, prepared to listen to what this sword had to say.

"My lady, when I was a simple young man, my grandmother had gifted me this sword, and I became a happy lad. My days were filled with childlike innocence as I learned the skill of swordsmanship. I spent my time in practice, and as I turned the ripe age of eighteen, it was my turn to become a soldier. As a soldier, I rose through the ranks of the military, and I knew that it was the sword that helped me! It was the sword that bolstered my ranks. When it was in my hands, I felt like the king, I felt like I was the one to be worshipped! I began to overly cherish it—you could have said that I may have revered it. If any other man's eyes were on my sword, I would raise *hell*. My sword was mine; it was mine!"

I flinched at the raised voice. The hairs on my arms stood on end. It continued talking. "It drove me crazy, but it was the key to my success. The narcissism began to eat at my insides. I was the best because of this cursed sword. It made me into who I was, who I had become. Alas, the day came for me to fight against the wicked army of Trunsia. That was the day that my sword failed me. I did not die, no, but as the killing blow was delivered to my unprotected scalp, the sword glowed blue, and in the next second, I found myself trapped within a dimly lit room. My lady, I was trapped within this desolate prison for eons! The sword, in its evil glory, told me that my only hope was a beautiful woman with flowing blond hair. It told me that she would be the one to finally take me away from this terrible predicament, that she would be my savior, if only she completed three tasks. My lady, you would do it, wouldn't you?"

My heart softened as I listened to the swordsman tell me of his struggles, but of what benefit was it to me if I helped him? As if he could hear what I was thinking, the swordsman said, "It offers a reward, one wish of your choice. Please, my lady, please, save me."

My eyes widened—a wish! Any wish, anything I wanted! This could be a dream come true! I mean, if the sword could trap someone inside of it, then of course it could grant my wish.

"Okay, okay, I'll do it! But first, tell me why you destroyed my home!" I yelled with a little bit of insanity. I had a right to be angry, my place was in shreds!

"My lady, you are surely one of the most generous." I smiled at that. Of course I was. "And it was this cursed sword that damaged your living quarters. I have no power over it, it just transported me here and proceeded to make havoc of your home. My deepest apologies, my lady."

"What about those holes in my yard? What are those for?"

"That is what I am just about to tell you," the swordsman said in a somewhat condescending tone. I dismissed it, my eyes on the prize. Of course, his explanation sort of made no sense, but it was the last thing I was thinking about, with a wish on the line.

"First, you must place your hand on the hilt of this cursed sword and repeat the oath of the swordbearer after me, then you must take this sword and chop off pieces of your beautiful blond hair and place them into the holes in your yard (which were the only things I made with my own intention), and lastly, you must find a living object to switch roles with me. This life will be switched with mine, and I will finally receive the freedom for which I have pined away for years and years. I will finally be free as a result of your generosity and your virtue, my lady," he stated with pure conviction. I could see his dark eyes, full of sincerity, staring deeply into my own, expressing such thankfulness that

I could feel the gratitude in my bones. (Not literally, of course, he was in a sword.) *I guess I'm his Princess Charming,* I thought to myself.

"Let's begin," I said, only thinking of my reward.

Without hesitation, he stated, "I vow to relieve the burden of the trapped entity within, and to protect it with my own generosity, by relieving the burden of the sword."

This oath I repeated, with my hand pressed onto the flat part of the blade. I could feel the cool metal and the words etched onto the surface. I wondered what they meant. I hesitated when I had to cut my beautiful blond hair, then just snipped off the tiny bits at the bottom, which fell into my palm like feathers that a fleeing bird would shed. I took a deep breath and pinched a bit of the pieces into the eight holes that had been made in the pristine grass of my backyard. Looking curiously at them, I noticed that there was a systematic order to their appearance, as if the swordsman had known that I would comply with his request. Shrugging it off, I finished placing bits of my hair into the holes, and grabbed the sword by its hilt.

"How am I supposed to find a living object?" I asked. "I'm not evil enough to trap something in here." There should be another option; why fix one life at the expense of another?

"Do not fear, my lady, I said that you may use *any* other living thing."

Ohhh, I get it! I could use a plant! That was living, right? Yes, yes it was. I grinned and ran into the house to grab one of my cacti. It was a young one, so I wouldn't notice its absence. After all, everything would be worth it when I got my wish. I could have *everything* that I desired with one wish. A delirious smile covered my face.

"Yes, yes, my lady! That is perfect, now please, stand in the middle of these potholes, put your hand on this sword while holding your plant, and say, 'Switch,'" the swordsman said a bit impatiently, but I didn't catch it in his voice, I was too busy daydreaming.

I took a deep breath, and thinking of my wish, I yelled with fervent passion, "*Switch!*"

Immediately I felt movement, and the ground crumbled beneath my feet. I fell into a deep pit, and there was darkness all around me. *Where was my wish!?* I looked up in panic, and looking down above me, with a sword in his hand, was a thin, withered old man with a wicked grin and braided black hair. He smirked, "Fell for it, didn't ya, my sweet? Ya fell for it, ya loony!" He grinned, showcasing a row of damaged teeth, yellowing and rotten. "Only a fool would fall for that, only a fool, oh, you fool, you fool! Didn't ya read the words on the sword? Didn't ya? Now it's your turn to suffer for a thousand years, you absolute fool!"

Tears filled my eyes as he banished me into the deep prison of the sword, where I would reside for a thousand years. Only a fool like me would fall for a dirty trick like that.

ANNIE HOANG

Of Metaphors, Monsters, and Wild Thoughts

People are made of glass. We are fragile and beautiful and when we break, our jagged edges spill blood on those who try to gather the pieces. We are born with hearts so thin, they shatter at the hand of others, and over time we find ourselves mending cracks and building walls. Our chests are two-way mirrors. People only make an effort to look because they see their own reflections staring back. The demons inside are invisible to the selfish human eye. No one knew that I carried a militia of monstrosities inside me. Not until they shattered me into a thousand incandescent shards.

Pain did not seem to be pain when you were empty. It was a whitewashed creature, really, a forgotten myth that stood on the line between the things I wanted and the things I dreaded. Never did Pain do much to harm me, rather it just held a presence. A presence that drove fear into the hearts of all kids. Big kids. Little kids. Kids who wore masks labeled ADULT to hide the person beneath. I was a kid in the middle, and though there were a million things about myself that were mysteries, I knew one thing for sure. Metaphors made up my world. Stories were a part of my world too, they were wild thoughts built on a foundation of metaphors. The Greeks were a metaphor for the creature called Pain in my Trojan Horse of Emptiness. Except in this story, the hatch to release them was undoubtedly glued shut, and the Greeks inside were stuck inside the wooden horse for all of eternity. While the Greeks played card games in their Trojan Horse of Emptiness, left on the outside world was my soul, unsure whether to celebrate the absence of Pain or prepare for battle. I wonder how many games of BS you could play in an eternity before you knew another person's lies as well as your own. I didn't even understand my own lies. The Greeks were a part of me and so was the Trojan Horse, and I had convinced myself that it was a harmless statue, maybe even a gift. Lying to myself was a bad habit, but it was how I hoped to survive. I told myself that the Trojan Horse was better than being hurt. I convinced myself that maybe feeling empty was better than feeling horrible. Being numb meant you didn't feel pain, and I lived in a world thriving on anesthetics. *Everyone* lied to avoid hurting, but I knew lies couldn't save me when the Trojan Horse provided a battle far worse than the Greeks ever could have. The Empty made everything with a point dull. It became the center of my universe and muted the colors of my existence. It coated memories in film, making them hard to see and impossible to feel. Life seemed to go by with me watching through a dirty windshield. Pain had been a birthright given to every human being. I could deal with pain. The Empty was different; it came to most but only stayed for some. The Empty was the first of the Monsters to haunt me, and I had thought it would be the only one. But I soon learned that this wasn't that simple. This was an army of Monsters, all lined up to take a shot at my mind. I fought hard enough. I kept them at bay, and maybe my efforts were about as successful as Sisyphus's, but here I was, undefeated. It was only when more started appearing that I knew I was in for trouble.

A group of crows is called a murder, and the Crows in my mind had plenty to kill. There was never a first day with them. It occurred more gradually. I had no memory without them, just as I had no memory of them coming. One by one they arrived, at first a silent whisper and growing to become a roaring wave. I had become their chosen target and it seemed like they never went to rest. I was followed everywhere by their loud presence, and I was the only one who could hear it. The Crows had feathers weaved in dark thoughts, slick and pitch-black, blending in with the shadows of nighttime. When they beat their wings, it brought down flurries of negativity to bitter my mind. Their beady black eyes stared back at me in the mirror, running judgmental looks across my body. *You're a waste of space,* they said. I shouldn't have listened, but if dark thoughts were the element of their feathers, then their claws were made of lies. They lacerated my outer skin and infused my blood with their lies. I chose to believe them. Not entirely, but for the most part, and that was what wounded me. The Crows were Monsters, but they were also wake-up calls and they seemed to call me out on every action I made. *Why would you do that? Why would you say that? You're so stupid.* It seemed like they were a part of me, like I had taken a piece of my mind and buried it a long time ago and it had come to return home. But at the same time the Crows felt wrong. Like someone had changed that part of me before allowing it to return. I had become an experiment, and the people who had concocted this change continued to do so with others. *Wow, procrastinating again. I really am not surprised.* My Crows were different than the ones that haunted my neighbor, and we both bore the weight of them alone. *What's the point of getting up, anyway? It's not like today will be different from tomorrow.* I wanted them to be quiet, to be gone in a way that I felt done with them but not vanquished from a part of myself. Similar to the rest of the world, I had no idea how to achieve this. *Do you really think anyone cares what you think? Yeah, didn't think so.* We were all aware that there were unwanted Crows flapping around each other. The problem was that we never attempted to silence them with shared conversations. I never made an attempt to quiet my Crows, even when I knew I had the capability to do so. It was too difficult to trust people with my problems in a world that treated others' problems like it did global warming. With practiced ignorance.

Zombies were everywhere. And not in a good way. Now, you may be questioning how Zombies could invade the world in an acceptable fashion, and to that I will hypocritically warn you not to lie to yourself. I know you've thought about the positives of a Zombie apocalypse at least once. Now, in any given situation of such, I would've wanted to take the role of badass resistance fighter, but being a badass resistance fighter meant that there was a resistance in the first place. In the cesspool known as high school, resistances were ants stomped on by the boot of social conformity before they would amount to anything near rebellion. That was what I had hoped, at least, that there had been something to squish in the first place. Most days I was left wondering exactly how alone I could claim to be. I knew I felt alone enough for it to hurt. Was I the only one immune? Or was it

about self-preservation? About staying you, even when everyone
and everything told you that being you meant being something
terrible. Zombies were mindless creatures, following one another
but having no real direction. The Crows may have deafened my
hope, but it was better than being brain-dead. I didn't want to
be like them, pretending that it was okay to accept the boxes we
were placed in at birth. There was something grand and melan-
choly to me about thinking of life so differently than the others did. I walked the halls listening to Zombie groans and never
quite understanding them, but hearing them clear as day. It was
surprisingly easy to talk to the Undead. They might've been the
only Monsters to appear outside my mind, but that didn't mean
they were hard to deal with. *Raaawwwwgggg* might've been lost
in translation, but I could bullshit my way through it as easily as
I did Spanish. The Undead existed without the need to harm
me, but it seemed they did it anyway. Being alone was supposed
to mean you wouldn't get hurt, but I learned that being alone
might've been what hurt the most. The Undead had a strangely
coveted version of happiness found in being together. And I
guess that's what I wanted most of all. To be happy.

I woke up one day realizing that not everyone had a beast
dwelling inside them. Not everyone woke up with clawing desolation stirring in their stomachs. And not everyone had a somber
ballad echoing their footsteps, making music a thing of despair
and desolation. That was the thing about the Beast, it was invisible to anyone without the right eyes. We are born blind, and it
seems to take too long for most people to realize they haven't
really been seeing at all. Realizations were terribly honest things,
my conscience decided. There is a beast dwelling inside me and
no one else in the entire world is forced into accepting the same
tenancy I am. The Beast invaded my body with no intent on leaving. It is wrecking my mind in its wake. It works in the wee hours
of the night, sending bad thoughts to my mind and causing me
to curl up into a ball in an effort to stop them. Its claws were
sharp as it padded around my aching body, and the bristles of
the Beast's fur tattooed hopelessness into my chest. Yet still I
woke up another day realizing that I did not hate the Beast as I
should have. The problem I had with it was the fact that I knew it
wasn't a diabolical villain. The Beast might've been the worst of
them all because it was made up of despair and an instinct that

longed to survive. We had too much in common. It was a desperate creature, only wishing to survive, even if that meant feeding off someone as vulnerable to the world as everyone else. I feared that looking in the mirror meant staring at the Beast. I feared that I had become the Beast, that it would be all I ever was. We were fighting a war over my body. One that would not end until one of us dropped down and died. Despite how long I have gone, I worried that one day I would lay down my weapons and hand myself over to the darkness. A battle raging against yourself was worst of all. It meant that no one saw your struggles because they existed only inwardly. There wasn't any bleeding, so there was no need for a bandage. But not all wounds can be treated that simply, and not all people know that they need to be treated at all. You can't see depression bleeding, it doesn't wound the body but the soul instead.

I had a list of Fears. They weren't Monsters, but they didn't hesitate to be there whenever the Empty haunted my nights and the Crows became too loud or when the Undead invaded my space and when the Beast became too hard to bear. My Fears were what weaved the Monsters into the same fate. They were the reason I was stuck in the eternal loop of bearing the Monsters.

1. Admitting to myself people could smile so effortlessly and never understand how I felt.
2. Failing so deep into a hole that I could never find a way out.
3. Getting infected by the metaphorical Zombie virus.
4. Being a useless Homo sapiens in a world moving at a speed I could never catch up to.
5. Loneliness.
6. Silence.
7. Losing my mind.

That was all I would like to share on the matter of Fears. My soul was hardly an open door; even the Monsters waging war could not win against the defenses keeping it closed.

The fact of the matter was that I knew I shouldn't have been fighting alone, but something kept me grounded to the Monsters. I feared silence more than I feared them. Silence meant thinking too much and thinking too much meant wanting to think nothing at all. I never had a pick, but I always knew that

there would be only one to come after me. One Monster over
another, but never all at the same time, and I guess that's what
caused my downfall on that day, the element of surprise. It was
the Struggle. The moment when the Monsters decided they were
tired of waiting in line. I was in the car on the way home from
school. It had been a bad couple of weeks. Weeks that were filled
by the Undead nearly swallowing me up in the classroom. Weeks
where I felt the Beast and the Empty churning in my stomach,
where the Crows had cawed incessantly and my Fears ran thick
through my blood. The Monsters had given up waiting, they had
all come closing in on me at once. Were the Monsters a perpet-
ual presence in my life? It had taken a lot of self-control to keep
things together, but sitting in the backseat listening to carpool
voices talk about such simple things made me snap. Cruel words
slide from the lips easier than apologetic ones do. Retreating
home meant that I could escape. Being alone didn't mean the
same as feeling alone, and sitting on the porch swing by myself
helped me to breathe a sigh of relief. And then came something
I thought would never come.

Hope.

It happened so quickly that I barely caught the shift. There
was a peach tree growing on the edge of the fence that separated our house from the neighbor's. From the convergence a
flock of small birds emerged. Something about watching them
fly changed me. The sky was a symphony of lilac and tangerine.
The scent of summer wafted in the air, despite the season being
months away, and there was something serene about the way everything swayed in the warm breeze. I watched the little birds flap
their wings as they passed overhead. For a moment, their bodies
were left suspended in the air before getting caught under the
beat of their wings. It was mesmerizing. The Wild Thoughts, the
good thoughts I hadn't known existed, came rushing toward the
Monsters at full force. The Empty was filled with colors made
from creativity, infused by music and magic and all things imag-
inable. The Crows were silenced by laughter, unadulterated, free-
spirited, giggle-until-your-sides-ache laughter. The Undead were
swept away by golden memories, dipped in liquid joy, delivering
the message *You are not alone.* If my struggles were Monsters, then
stories were Warriors. The Wild Thoughts rampaged through the
darkness, filling warmth where shadows lurked and painting the

streets of my mind in vibrant colors. I wanted to listen to their music, music that was filled with colors instead of shadows, and I longed to breathe in air instead of smoke. So I did. I did because I could. Because the Wild Thoughts were real and they outweighed the Monsters. The Monsters were yet to be tamed and things were yet to be okay but I knew they would be. I knew it with every fiber of my being. Maybe things weren't perfect, and maybe there were days when the Monsters would roar louder than the Wild Thoughts, but I knew that the sun would rise and I would try again. We would try again. I wasn't alone anymore, and I didn't want to be. I had a choice. Zombies could become friends. And old friends didn't cease to exist the moment you were separated. Thoughts about my loved ones filled my heart, gave me the strength to keep pumping. South of my heart, the Beast roamed, but it seemed that a hibernation was in store. Happiness is what filled you up when the well in your soul had been sucked dry. I would be happy, piece by piece, day by day. Until my soul felt full again. The Monsters were what haunted me, but the Wild Thoughts were what drove me to keep fighting.

Arasing

TURNING THE CORNER past the tin-roofed temporary buildings, you find a body of bees walking the labyrinth. They—it? —stroll meditatively, each step a humming cloud of yellow and black, hands clasped together so that the arms seem to be a looping stream of activity, bees dodging each other in the deltoid, bouncing down the biceps, swimming along what you would guess to be the extensor carpi ulnaris, but Greg only lets you look at his anatomy textbook for five minutes at a time because he says your little English-major brain wouldn't be able to handle all the information, so you're not sure.

The body, Greg likes to say, *holds the secrets of the world.* Greg, wet granite eyes and copper cleft chin, knows many secrets.

Today he told you:

1. In high school there was this chick Angie little Argentinian firecracker called me *picaflor* but I didn't care her waist was so small I could wrap my hands around it and have the fingers touch.

2. Stop coughing Joseph breathe think about this while you are inhaling so are your cells but exhaling too it's faster than you can imagine it's called cellular respiration there are tiny flickers of motion and exchange within your lungs within your everywhere can you believe that can you believe the miracles happening right now inside you if you learn enough it's almost like there are no miracles at all.

3. Oh and Angie yeah that chick she'd make me sing "Angie"

to her every night Angie Angie Angie until she fell asleep she
loved the Stones she'd get goose bumps that's called arasing,
the muscles under each follicle contract I still think about
that like a braille of attraction.
4. So who's the poet now Joseph?

You said he had some talent.
He said there's no such thing. Only practice.
You said training to be a surgeon is different and your voice
trailed off so of course the question:
Different from what?
You were too high to argue so you giggled and then everyone
giggled for a while.

And then Greg said, his eyes glazing into doughnut holes under the afternoon smoke, that there was a labyrinth tucked away
somewhere on campus. Greg said that he himself had tucked the
labyrinth in and sang it to sleep sometimes but Greg always talks
about his mommy issues when he's stoned so you said *Stop right
there Greg, let's go find the labyrinth, let's go right now.*

Greg agreed, but he ditched you seven minutes ago at Jenny's
dorm because Jenny had just come back from volleyball practice
and was slimy like an oyster on the half shell and Greg had the
munchies and how could you expect him to resist that anyways,
they don't even wear pants you know. So it was just you walking
the route that soon-to-be-Dr. Greg had prescribed, past the en-
vironmental issues majors sitting in the trees *K-I-S-S-I-N-G*, past
the European-history professor and his furtive student lover, past
the freshmen sobbing into their calculus textbooks. Two marine
biologists explored each other's tentacular tendencies and you
thought lazily of Jenny and Greg, entangled in her dorm.

You thought does Jenny know about Angie from Argentina
and does Jenny like the Stones. And does he give Jenny goose
bumps. And is Jenny satisfied. And could Jenny ever love you.
And you were sinking toward dangerous deep-sea thoughts so
you rose back to the surface.

Jenny is textbook beautiful (you suspect that's the reason she
holds Greg's attention), legs up to your ears and prone to the
kind of crass wisecracks that pretty girls make when they're used
to being used. She bites her lip when she's thinking. She chews
on pencil erasers. You wonder if she would still do these things if

she wasn't always watched. You want to ask Greg if she does that around him, but that would mean he'd be watching her, so your question gets all tangled inside you and you quit.

You wonder how long one must be loved before a stare stops feeling foreign. Maybe never.

Greg and Jenny are almost something. She hovers around their dorm like an uneasy, elegant insect, folding their laundry and making their beds. She sleeps with him dutifully and answers his constant phone calls with a stoic, almost motherly patience. You, the roommate, are chief witness to their near-being.

You won't pretend you don't find Jenny attractive. As a matter of fact, half of your and Greg's conversations revolve around the two of you finding Jenny attractive—it's one of the few commonalities between you. But Greg is the only one who can give firsthand accounts of her breasts, so he has the power. You both know that. You both know that.

It's not like you don't stare at her a lot. Maybe more than you should. But she has these magic thighs—long, tan, softer than a baby's ass Greg says. Sometimes you try and think of things softer than those thighs. You imagine the thighs on a sheepskin rug, the thighs kicking through the clouds, the thighs shining in a pool of velvety honey. Magic thighs. Greg likes to wrap one hand around them at parties, on the dorm couch, while driving. You'd think simply resting a hand on a thigh wouldn't be a driving hazard, but Greg claims the magic thighs distract him from the road, that his vision swims on contact, that's just how magic they are. You asked whether his books had any kind of anatomical explanation for this phenomenon and he called you a wiseass and never gave an answer, which you took as a kind of victory, your romantic sensibilities triumphing over science. A tiny triumph for you to mark up against all his territorial thigh touches.

One day, *you're* going to touch those thighs. You're going to reach out as she sails by and run one finger down the smoothness of those thighs and she'll rip her clothes off and tackle you in a soft and yearning fashion and Greg will spontaneously combust. It's a nice thought.

But right now, for the first time in months, you're not weighing the risks and rewards of touching Jenny's thighs. You're face-to-face with a bee man. You take a half step toward the bees, and a whole step back. You consider doing the hokey pokey.

It's the ambiguity here that scares you. If it's a man made of bees then when you say hello it might wave or buzz back or ask you for directions to the dorms because it's very lost and something terrible has happened. But if it's a bunch of bees making up a man—that's a whole different story. They might turn on you. They might drop the pretense and expand into a vicious swarm.

The man stops and looks up. Its face shifts in a way that could be a smile, or a baring of teeth, or a grimace. You wave like it's a baby, opening and closing your fist. It raises its arm, a club of bees curling into a ball and then exploding out. The hand expands and contracts a few times, and a line of yellow and black snakes out of the rippling rib cage, landing gently on you. You're mesmerized and statue-still but can't resist laughing when the bees arrange themselves on your arm. Their tiny feet tickle. They spell *H-E-L-L-O*.

"Hello," you say.

I AM BENJAMIN.

"Benjamin. I'm Joseph."

JOSEPH.

"Yes."

The bees have dropped just slightly out of formation, their humanoid figure dripping at the edges. You stand, the bees trembling on your skin, feeling your image refracting through thousands of compound eyes. It must seem like there's a swarm of you too.

"So." How to ask for a backstory. You dizzy your brain searching for subtlety.

SO. The bees wriggle in the *O*; you can almost hear the intonation of expectation.

"Can you. Um. Do you sting?" A reasonable question.

YOU MUST NOT TAKE BIO.

"Ha, well, no, actually, I'm focusing on English . . ."

MAKES SENSE.

Pause.

WALK WITH ME.

You step into the labyrinth, eyes on your arm, and follow Benjamin along the calming curves.

1 STING = 1 DEAD BEE.

You nod.

I DON'T GET THEM BACK.
"Oh."
You've reached the center. Benjamin faces you, the sun glinting off his many wings like glass.
"What do you study?"
BUSINESS.
"Nice."
Suddenly, your arm is bare. Benjamin whirls into a column and solidifies, bees blurring into bone structure, skin stretching over the shaking mass, until a blond, bright-eyed boy in a black T-shirt sits with his arms wrapped loosely around his knees.
"Sorry if I startled you," Benjamin says.
"Uh-huh."
"The labyrinth calms me down, y'know. Helps me reconstruct. You may want to keep that in mind."
"What?"
"It'll happen to you too, someday."
"What?"
"True emotion." Benjamin shakes his head and smiles. "Shit's insane." He stands up haphazardly, and giggles as he walks past you. "Gets me every time."
You sway in the center of the labyrinth, watching him walk away. A fly lands on your shoulder. You jump and brush it off.
In high school you wrote love letters to Sarah Anderson every second Tuesday of the month. They said things like *You are like the sun to me* and *I long for you like a compass needle to the North Pole* and toward the end *Loving you has been like slaving over a meal for someone else to eat,* which, although not your finest work, gave the most satisfaction when you slipped it in her locker. Your head squeezes for a second. True emotion. Unlikely.
If you were to write Jenny a letter, you think maybe it would say:

Hello Jenny it's Joseph every time I see you I get hunger pangs I've heard of heartache but not craving someone like this I wonder if you're sweet did you know that Greg compares you often to caramel in a way I find quite unappealing why do you love him do you shave or wax your legs or are you naturally hairless like one of those goblin cats would you like to read my poetry there aren't too many love poems and none of them are about you anyways you're at the bottom of my trigger list quite a few guns will have to go off before I get to you.

Benjamin may have startled you a little. You weave your brain tissue back together, remember punctuation. It puts tidy little snaps between your words, straightens them out like a hammer and anvil.

You need to find Greg. The walk back to Jenny's is a daze and all of a sudden you're hesitating at the door to her room, realizing you've never been to her place before. You test the knob. It's unlocked. Some part of you must know what you're going to walk into, because you don't even consider knocking. Some part of you must want to see Jenny and Greg molding together under her cheap yellow sheets.

The half second between when you first glimpse their figures and when they hear the door creak lasts for years. Jenny's head is thrown back, chapped lips parted, eyes closed. Her hair sprawls across the pillow, her hand in the process of loosening its hold on the mattress, turning palm up, almost inviting you in as Greg plants a gentle kiss on the underside of her jaw. You have time to wonder idly if his stubble tickles. His naked back has a long, thin scar running down the middle, a dull dry pink in contrast to his sweaty skin. Jenny's other hand spreads across his shoulder blades, moving ever so gently toward the line, like an eager car veering toward the center of an empty road.

That's what's most private about the moment, you think. The certainty of Jenny's hand moving to trace the scar. You've never seen it—you once heard Greg mention something about scoliosis, but assumed it was in reference to his studies. It seems impossible that Greg was once crooked.

As Greg's head begins to rise, sensing someone else in the room, something strange happens to Jenny's form. Her lips soften, spread into petals almost, and then flap away, rosy wings attached to tiny black bodies. Her skin splits into butterflies, the sheets collapsing over their thrumming thoraxes. Greg jumps back, taking the cover with him, and the remaining insects flee the room, rushing down the hall in a cloud of sunset reds, pinks, and oranges. Greg collapses onto the bed.

"Are . . . you okay?"

Greg doesn't even question why you're there. He stretches out a shaking hand. A butterfly is trapped between his fingers, one wing crumpled. Almost without thinking, he makes a fist. When he opens it again, a mangled purplish thing remains.

"Which part?"

"What?"

Which part which part which part. "Of Jenny. Where was your hand?"

"I dunno, her legs? Her thighs? I—Joseph, what was that?"

But you're halfway out the door already. Girls line the hall, looking after where the train of bugs must have left. Some shake their heads knowingly, others remain frozen in disbelief.

"Wait! What was that?" Greg calls after you. "Joseph!"

You keep going. You walk down the hall until you find a broom closet. You sit down inside.

Of course, it makes sense that Greg would be the one to give it to Jenny. Whatever the fuck it is. It makes sense that beautiful Greg, who can smoke without coughing, just broken enough to need saving but remain attractive, intelligent soon-to-be-surgeon Greg would give it. And it makes sense that he would keep a piece of the thighs for himself. That touching them all those times in front of you wouldn't be enough, that he'd have to hold just a little bit.

You see the thighs, Jenny's empty blue gaze, a future where you get to grip them whenever you want, where she would know your scars, where Greg would find you two in all the crudest positions possible, and he wouldn't be able to do a thing about it, because your tiny little brain and obsolete major would have finally gotten the girl. Even now, imagining the thighs, they look somehow chewed up. He took a piece.

You feel your face heating. You wanted to give it to her, whatever it was. The want pulls in your guts like a thousand high school tug-of-war teams that picked you last. You've never gotten the Jenny. Never been able to give it to her.

Your throat tightens, and as you raise your hand to rub away the tears sneaking out of your eyes, you glimpse one of your fingernails completing its metamorphosis into a shining jewel beetle.

S I M O N   L I U

All Westbound Trains

All westbound trains on track 1 have been delayed.

A SIGH COULD BE heard coming from just below the loud-speaker. There was effort behind it as it stretched out, taking care to ensure that the sole other occupant would note the exasperation behind it.

Montgomery wondered how just one sigh could irritate him to such a degree. Perhaps it was the unnatural length of it that turned the vibrations—just vibrations—to a fly that buzzed in his ear and speckled his vision. But Montgomery could not be annoyed by a sigh. The sigh was from a person, one that he could target his silent frustrations toward. He resisted, but unable to control the impulse, Montgomery stole another glance at the man with whom he shared the night clouds.

The man stood on the opposing platform with his back facing west, away from the direction his train would come from. The man's foot tapped a slow, inconsistent tempo—*tap*—the sound reverberating off the beams—*tap*—holding up the station over-hangs. Against the wall of ambient noise, they—*tap*—anchored Montgomery to reality, keeping his thoughts from drifting too far. The taps were time slowing down, signaling for him to hurry on. Montgomery looked away, letting his eyes glaze over until they became glassy.

All around him were the signs of nightfall as the wilderness came to life. Fireflies lit the countryside, which, excluding the railroad town, was almost empty of any development. Above them, stars were almost visible, but still indiscernible through the cloud cover. The breeze wafted the buzz of critters through the air and into the station. Montgomery imagined that the countryside would eventually give way—in perhaps fifty years—to a metropolis, that a population boom would create an urban center. He envisioned streets filled not with the buzz of crickets but the buzz of people—*tap*—. But for now, all that was there was an untouched rural landscape.

Montgomery gripped his ticket in his hand. The flimsy paper was bent and crumpled from his constant fumbling and folding. This two- by five-inch slip was Montgomery's getaway from the countryside he had squandered all his life in. He was discontent with this lifestyle, being so disconnected from the world out there. He was discontent with how his life seemingly repeated itself over again each day; it seemed as if he was just a constantly looping song on an old stereo. There was no living out here. People just went through the motions. He could not live like this any longer. Even so, it had happened all so suddenly; no time at all had been afforded to Montgomery to think about his future. He was still unsure about it all; he had been unsure about it for a long time now.

But he had received an escape to a greater story: a ticket out. And he was taking a leap. He wanted to become someone, something that could not be done here, for nothing could ever be done here. This was not a place where people were able to do things. This was a place where people rigged time to never move forward but instead trap their souls in a cycle of daily living. This was a place where discontinued automatons, having been replaced with newer models, came to die. Montgomery had to go out there and so he had gotten a ticket. No goodbyes were needed; Montgomery had no friends or family left that would come after him if he left. He had been here for too long, as no one he knew still remained. Those who had wanted more in their lives had long since left, walked to the same train station he now stood in and gone either east or west. It didn't matter. It just had to be somewhere else. The train station was the last anyone leaving saw of their town—of their past life. There would be no return visits with their reflections of sentiment, if only because Montgomery had no sentiment of his hometown. And reassured that this was the only right course, he let himself return to his surroundings— *tap*—.

There, as if acknowledging Montgomery's attention, the air began to buzz with electricity just as a rush of warm wind was being carried around the tracks, signaling the arrival of an incoming eastbound passenger train. While Montgomery recognized it as not his train, it was comforting nonetheless. Its presence filled up the empty space while light shining from the windows brushed away the gloom. Warmth flooded into the station, not only through the feel of the air, but into the painted colors— grays becoming oranges and dulls becoming brights. And having completed its transformation of the station, the train eased to a stop. A low whistle bellowed out.

Montgomery felt soothed, as if the warmth evaporated what worries he had had about starting anew in a different world entirely. He wished he could remain this way forever, bathed in the glow of a new future, but still free of the worries that came with such a major change. Now being covered by the protective shadow of the locomotive, Montgomery took the time to notice things. The pistons underneath the train thrust up and down with a rhythm, producing the unmistakable sound of a steam engine, its hiss. But even with an engine, the aura rising from the bells and whistles of the train looked as if it could power the train alone. He was truly alone in the train station as the man had become hidden behind the train and Montgomery questioned whether the man was there anymore. He was the only one on this platform, in this train station; he was the only one who was even awake this time of night. He was the only one left who had the dream to escape this town.

And thinking to himself, Montgomery found that he was envious of the passengers in the train. He was envious that they, in their shared mirth together, knew where they were going. The passengers on the train knew their destinations; they knew of how it would end. And they had all known this before him. Montgomery did not have the solace of certainty; he had no plan for the next chapter to his own life, much less any endings. He had only the hope of making it work. Fate would not give him aid; it had never done so in the past. He would have to fight for a new life.

Montgomery, certain that his mind had finally been made up, allowed himself to lean back on the beam. He breathed out and let his mind dance away with the lights from the train windows, which traced out silhouettes of the passengers. Before long, the train blew another whistle and the pistons started speeding up, going faster, faster, faster, until with a flourish, the train cleared the station. The lights were gone now, as were the restful sounds of the train. Then, looking at the opposite platform, Montgomery noticed the other man had also been whisked away by the train's departure.

And while his only companion was gone, the warmth still remained. The pleasant thoughts that had reassured him before had remained, their roles still not finished. But it would not be much longer. It could only be some while until with gusto, his train would sweep into the station just as the last had. It too would pump its pistons up and down, a gentle hiss coming out once it had pulled to a stop. The doors would glide open and Montgomery would board, and then the train would take Montgomery onward. He would finally do this.

It would just be a little longer. His train was just delayed. All westbound trains were.

AELA MORRIS

A Portrait of the Artist
as a Teenage Girl

EVERYTHING ABOUT THE NEW HOUSE felt wrong. Lying in
the darkness, I feel it seeping into me. The heater sounds like
a monster rising from the deep . . . *Crash!* Realizing how close I
had been to sleep, I clamber out of bed and tug open the window
to discover the source of this impromptu percussion show. My
bedroom window provides the perfect view of the house across
the street. It's a brick row house, same as all the others, but with
something foreboding about it. There isn't any specific reason
for this, it's just a feeling I have. Cobwebs where there shouldn't
be, strange shadows, you know. I glance around for a beat before
I find the source: somebody running from the house. They had
knocked over some flowerpots and triggered the streetlamps,
bathing the street in a yellow light, like the set of a film noir. And
then they're gone, just a smudge in a dark green sweatshirt on
the horizon line.

Things that happen in that hazy space between night and day
often seem less real—a half dream. So, the next morning, walking past the house, I was surprised to see a man picking up the
pot shards. He looked to be around my father's age, but his hair
had gone almost completely gray already, so maybe he was older.
I didn't recognize him from the stupid "Welcome New Neighbors" party my mom had dragged me to. I also don't realize that
I'm staring at him until, with a laugh, he says, "Someone really
doesn't like geraniums."

"I didn't think that anyone lived here," I say hurriedly, feeling
some need to explain my presence on the sidewalk.

"Just the way I like it. I like peace and quiet." He extends a hand. "I'm Charlie."

I shake it. "Sophie."

"Sophie," he says as if he is tasting the name. "The Greeks' word for 'wise.' No pressure." There's a twinkle in his eye. I grin in spite of myself, say goodbye, and start to walk away.

"Sophie!" Charlie calls after me. "I know a fellow artist when I see one." He's pointing at the black Moleskine sketchbook in my hands. I turn around, wanting to ask him what he means, but he's vanished inside the house.

I spend my entire first day at my new school with Charlie's words rolling around in my head. I bought the sketchbook in a gift shop somewhere in Michigan. It was the last family vacation we went on before my parents split up. My father found more happiness in books and petri dishes than in my mom and me. That's how we found ourselves here, living in an old house that my mom can "fix up" and fill with all the antique furniture she pleases. In a place where downtown only takes up two streets and there isn't a skyscraper to be seen. He would have hated it here. I hope I don't.

At lunch, I forgo the cafeteria and head to my tried-and-true strategy, the art room. If there's anyone in there, they usually keep to themselves. And if there's no one in there, it means that there's no one to see you eating alone. This particular art room has a boy with messy brown hair and a plain gray T-shirt.

"What are you doing?" he demands as I take a seat at the other end of the room. "You need to get out, now." He doesn't even give me time to answer the question.

"Why?"

"Because only *I* eat in here. Goodbye." He crosses the room and opens the door for me with mock politeness.

It's then that I look over to where his backpack is sitting and notice a very familiar green sweatshirt. "You! You were the one who broke all the pots at the house across the street from mine last night!"

"So what's your point? Looking to get me arrested for breaking and entering? Because I wasn't."

"No, I'm just interested to know what you're doing."

"Well, don't be, it's none of your business."

"Maybe I *will* call the cops then."

"Get. Out. Now."

And with that he gives me a shove and slams the door behind me.

"Asshole!" I shout at no one.

That afternoon, I somehow find myself standing on Charlie's front porch. He answers the door with a slightly amused expression on his face.

"What did you mean by 'fellow artist'?" I say before I lose my nerve.

Charlie smiles and gestures for me to follow him inside. We enter what is supposed to be the living room, but instead of a couch and coffee table, it's filled to bursting with canvases, paint, and children's books.

"You're an illustrator?" Charlie nods, smiling. Before I know what I'm doing, I pull out my own sketchbook.

Despite what he said about liking peace and quiet, Charlie doesn't seem to mind me hanging around. After school, I sit in the living room and watch him paint. Sometimes he has me cleaning brushes or organizing supplies. Other times we sit, baking in the sun, at his kitchen counter, and just talk. About art and politics, and my own drawings. I also complain about gray T-shirt kid, whose real name is Jack. We've had several run-ins since the lunch incident. Most of them involve arguments over art supplies and who gets to store their project where. It exasperates me. Charlie doesn't seem to have much sympathy, which is infuriating.

"The greatest artists are often misunderstood" is all he says every time I bring it up.

"You're just as bad as Jack," I mutter.

Later that week, I'm clearing up in the art room after class when I spot a sketchbook sitting next to the sink. I flip it open to the inside cover and see the words PROPERTY OF JACK LINCOLN. PLEASE RETURN and then an address. *His loss,* I think to myself, and move on. But then I think about what would happen if I lost my sketchbook. I sigh and grab it on my way out.

I find Jack's house easily, and a middle-aged woman bearing a striking resemblance to him answers the door.

"Are you a friend of Jack's?" she says in a way that makes me think Jack doesn't have many friends. She introduces herself as his mother and lets me in, talking a mile a minute.

"Jack's dad would have just loved you. He loved art just like you two. He was an illustrator . . ."

"What happened to him?" I'm feeling dizzy, and my voice sounds alien in my ears.

"Oh, he passed when Jack was eight. He had leukemia."

I'm not listening anymore; I'm staring at the mantel. On it sits a photograph of a man, around my dad's age, graying hair. "Charlie," I whisper.

"I'm sorry, I have to go!" I turn and run from the house, into the street, as the day turns into night, Jack's sketchbook still in my hands.

I reach Charlie's house in record time, and bang on the door. "Charlie! Charlie, please!" My voice becomes raw. No one responds. The door is locked. I run around the back, searching for another entrance. I spot a window slightly ajar, and climb inside. The house is deserted. The paintings, the books, the sunlit kitchen counter, they're all gone.

"*Charlie!*" I scream in vain, knowing there would be no answer. There never was one. *I'm crazy.* I sink to the floor, sobbing.

I lose track of time. Maybe hours pass, maybe only a few minutes, but eventually I hear footsteps.

"Sophie?" It's Jack. "What are you doing here? What's wrong?" He sits down beside me.

"I'm crazy. Your dad, I saw him, he was here. I talked to him every day for months. But he's dead, he's been dead for years."

Jack is quiet for a long time.

"What did he say?"

"Whatever my deranged mind thought he should."

"Sophie, you're not crazy. Maybe he was trying to send a message to us."

"You seriously believe that I received some kind of sign from above?" I almost laugh.

"I—when my dad was sick, everyone in the family shaved their heads, you know, in support. But I didn't. I was growing it out; I thought it made me look like a rock star. So we were all there, at the end, and he was reaching out and touching everybody's heads and he's smiling, the biggest smile he's had in weeks. And then he got to me, and he just kind of tousled my hair and didn't say anything. I think he was disappointed. So I just thought, maybe I could do it now, in our old house." He holds up an electric razor.

"Like a message to him." For once his eyes don't look disgusted or angry. They don't look friendly, either, more like they have the possibility of friendliness. Maybe it's why the next thing that comes out of my mouth is, "Do you want me to do it?" His voice says, "I guess, if you want to." His eyes just say yes. I follow him into the bathroom, which is dingy and smells like the bottom of a pond. The electricity is shut off, so there are no lights, just the two of us staring into the mirror in the dark.

"He was going to teach me to shave in here, when I was old enough," says Jack to no one in particular. I engage the razor and make the first cut. When we see the flesh-colored stripe in the center of Jack's wild crown of hair, we start to laugh in spite of ourselves.

When we're finished, we collapse on the tile floor. Jack absent-mindedly runs his hand across his newly shaved head. It's silent and the cold bathroom tiles are making my butt sore, but somehow I am more at peace here than in my own house. Reflected in the bathroom tiles in front of me is a blond head, staring back. I pick up the razor and place it, soundlessly, in Jack's hand.

"Are you sure?" His voice is barely there. I nod. As the cold metal makes contact with my head, I think about calling my father. Maybe I need to send a message too.

The Cabin

SHE AWOKE WITH A START, her heart pounding as if she had just outrun a storm. It was dark all around her, and for a moment she began to panic, thinking she was still dreaming. She sat bolt upright, gasping in cooling breaths, and jumped when a soft hand landed on her arm.

"Shh . . . just relax. You hit your head pretty hard."

She squinted in the darkness, but all she could see was the vague silhouette of a man. He had an amiable sort of voice, light and mellow, the kind that you instantly wanted to trust.

"Who are you?" she whispered.

"My name is Mark," said the voice, and she could hear the reassurance in it. "I found you out in the woods, unconscious. I think maybe you slipped and hit your head on a rock."

She lifted a hand and raised it to her forehead, wincing as she found a lump the size of an egg. "I don't even remember falling."

"Don't worry about it too much," Mark said, patting her arm. "The heat probably got to you. You'll be just fine." She heard a shuffling noise, and then felt something soft slide into place behind her back. "What's your name?" said Mark gently, fluffing the pillow up.

"Eleanor," she said, swallowing as her heartbeat began to regulate again. "Ellie."

"It's nice to meet you, Ellie," he said. "Why don't we get a bit of light in here, what do you say?"

She heard him get up (he must have had a chair by the bed) and move to the other side of the room. There was the noise of a drawer opening, the scratch of the match, and then light erupted from the tiny pinprick. He picked up a candle and lit it, shaking out the match as the flame fizzled out. "That's better," he said, raising the candle up to light up his face.

All at once, Ellie felt a sickening lurch in her stomach, something she couldn't quite place. All she knew was that something didn't feel right. Mark looked at her curiously, the candlelight illuminating his dark brown, almost black eyes and sandy blond hair that fell across his forehead in chunks.

"Is something wrong?" he said, watching her closely.

"No," said Ellie uncertainly. "I don't—have we met before?"

He looked puzzled. "I don't believe so. Why?"

"I just . . ." she said, hesitating. "I just thought I recognized you."

He shook his head. "I think I'd remember meeting you," he said, smiling.

"Oh?" said Ellie, arching an eyebrow as she struggled to get off the bed. "And why is that?"

He didn't reply, just smiled shyly. "Here, let me help."

He strode across the room and let her hold on to his arm as she heaved herself up. "Thank you," said Ellie, swaying slightly, "for that and for letting me rest here. But I really should get going."

"Got a boyfriend to get back to?" he said innocently enough, but she caught the connotation underneath.

"No boyfriend," she clarified, "just a cat who will be very angry with me if I don't get home in time to feed her."

"Well, eat something before you leave, at least. Just a little," he added as she began to protest. "One bowl of soup and then you can head on your way."

She hesitated, then smiled. "Alright. Thank you."

He released her and went over to the stove in the corner of what she was beginning to realize was a small log cabin. It was just one room, with the bed she had been sleeping on in one corner, a small sofa across from it, and the kitchen diagonal to the sofa. Ellie sat down at the table, wincing as her head throbbed horribly. She lifted her fingers to her temple again, and as she did the faintest vestige of a memory began to form in her mind's eye.

She could feel her heart pounding, sense the eyes following her through the trees. Twigs snapped behind her, and she quickened her pace, but the growing volume of the footsteps told her they were getting closer.

"Everything okay?"

She jumped, and the memory disappeared as quickly as it had come. Mark was scrutinizing her, his eyebrows knitting together.

"I think I remembered something," she said, biting her lower lip anxiously. "When you found me, was there anyone else around?"

"No, it was just you," he said. "Why?"

"I remember someone following me," she said quietly.

His expression changed, almost imperceptibly. "Are you sure?"

"Positive."

He turned away from her to open a can of soup, and for a moment the only noise was the grinding of the can opener. Then, as the can clinked open and he tipped the contents into a small pot, he said, "Maybe you shouldn't leave, then. What if whoever was following you comes back?"

Ellie shook her head. "I'm sure it'll be fine. It was probably just another hiker. Maybe I overreacted."

"Maybe." He didn't say anything more, just ladled soup into two mismatched bowls. "Dinner is served," he said, sticking a spoon in one bowl and offering it to Ellie.

"Thanks," she said, inhaling the rich tomato scent.

"So," said Mark, sitting down opposite her with his own bowl, "what were you doing in the woods? Just hiking?"

"Actually, I'm a photographer," said Ellie as she swallowed a mouthful of soup. "Well, amateur photographer. Anyway, I went looking for some new inspiration. Now that I think of it," she said suddenly, glancing around her, "have you seen my camera? It was the only thing I had on me."

"I picked it up," he said, smiling. "It's in my bag." He nodded behind her, and she turned to find a brown knapsack on the side table by the bed. "I figured you wouldn't want to lose it."

"Thank you," she said, relieved. "I was afraid it was gone forever."

They ate in silence for a few minutes, and Ellie found herself glancing around the cabin. It was fairly minimalistic, but in the corner by the door there was a small rack filled with various hammers, ropes, and knives.

"This is my hunting cabin," said Mark, noticing where she was looking.

"Strange hunting weapons," she commented, glancing over at him.

He smiled, and something in it seemed slightly inhuman. "I hunt strange prey," he said, but he didn't elaborate, and she didn't ask.

She stared at the rack again, something struggling to connect in her mind. "That hammer," she said, suddenly remembering. "The one with the orange handle. I've seen it before."

"I don't doubt that," he said, laughing. "It was five dollars at Home Depot. Probably everyone you know has one just like it. Can I take your bowl?"

She handed it to him wordlessly, and as he headed to the sink, she retrieved her camera from his knapsack. She pushed the on button and it booted up, taking her to her saved pictures. She began to flip through them, recognizing the close-ups of squirrels and flowers she had snapped on her hike. As she clicked through picture after picture, she noticed that they were getting shakier. There was one of the ground that must have been accidentally taken as she was running.

Then, all of a sudden, a familiar face stared up at her. It was contorted in fury, dark eyes boring into her and sandy blond hair wildly blown over his forehead. Her heart began to hammer in her chest as the memory came back all at once.

She was racing through the trees, her breath coming out in short gasps. Her camera banged against her chest in rhythm with her pounding heart, and as she ran she heard his footfalls grow closer and closer. Then his hand clamped around her arm, and as the orange hammer came down, her fingers slipped across her camera. She heard the click of the shutter, and then all she could do was scream before the awful pain sent her spiraling into darkness.

"You shouldn't have done that."

Her heart seemed to still in her chest, and she sucked in a breath as she whirled around to face him. His jaw was set, his eyes like dark tunnels. Before she could think to move, he had snatched the camera out of her hands.

"It was you," she whispered, swallowing hard. "You were the one chasing me. You *kidnapped* me."

He sighed. "I really hoped it wouldn't come to this, Ellie." He made a move toward her, but she dived out of the way, streaking toward the door, running faster than she ever had in her life. But just as her hand closed around the handle, he seized her around the stomach and flung her backward. She screamed as she fell, flailing out; her foot hit the weapons rack and tools came tumbling down. She heard Mark's grunt of pain as the rack fell on top of him, and she tried to scramble away, but his hand closed around her ankle and yanked her back toward him.

She felt herself being flipped over, and then she was staring straight into his black eyes. His forehead was bleeding where the rack had hit it, and his face was contorted in a snarl. "You can't run," he said, his breath hot on her ear. "You think you're the first to try? I've brought a dozen other women here. None have escaped. Well," he said, laughing low in his throat, "not alive, anyway."

She struggled to get away, but he pinned her arms down with his legs. "Any last words?" he sneered, panting.

Her frantic fingers closed on something thick and heavy. "Yeah," she gasped. *"Go to hell."*

She swung her arm up, ripping it out of his grasp, and the hammer in her hand drove home into his skull. There was the crunch of metal on bone, and then his expression went slack and he collapsed on top of her, his dead weight heavy on her chest. She flung him off and scrambled to her feet, nearly slipping in the rapidly growing pool of blood. She stared at the hammer, hardly able to believe it was her hand holding it. For a moment she almost regretted it; then she took a shaky breath, dropped her camera around her neck, and left the cabin without a glance back, the dripping hammer still hanging from her limp fingers.

JOSHUA PECK

Etiam Doloris

EVERYONE DIES, and it ultimately becomes the responsibility of those who live on to decide what to make of that life. As for hers, well, I don't know really. After all these years and all that pain, I should know her as well as I know myself, but I don't. Yet, I can say one thing with absolute certainty: she had the most painful life of anyone I have ever known, but you can be the judge of what it amounted to.

As I stand here, at the foot of a grave I never wanted to see. I remember her life, all the time we spent together, all the things I didn't do for her, all the words I never said. I cry out, scream, rage at the sky itself even as it bursts out a clap of thunder in reply.

I sink to my knees and weep, the fear, anger, loss, and grief of the past few days, weeks, and years finally hitting me. I suppose I look very much like a child, my fists clenching the dirt and my face buried in the soil as tears stream down my face, to drip down into the earth and become some part of new life.

With my tears drying in the dirt, I can't help but be reminded of another time, another place, when I watched someone else crying, just like I am now. It was the first time I had ever seen her.

She was eight years old, kneeling in her front yard, hands squeezing the earth in her knotted-up little fists. The shouting from inside the house is what caught my attention, two people, I assumed they were her parents, were going at it. Yelling and screaming, arguing with a ferocity that displayed their naked hate. For all that noise you would think such a small girl would cover her ears, but she didn't, she just kept on squeezing the dirt until her knuckles turned white and the grains of sand and stones left imprints in her palms. Then she let go, not because of the pain, but by a change in volume from the house. The arguing had stopped, now only one voice yelled; the other was quiet but for occasional screams of pain and anguish. That's when the girl's forehead dropped to the ground, her tears simply water for whatever may live in the dirt.

At the time, I was only seven years old; I could not grasp the gravity of the situation, or even describe it like I do now. But a child can understand much that an adult cannot, maybe that's why I did what I did. If I were to witness a similar situation now, when I am much much older, I would not act with such wisdom as I did all those years ago, unintentional as it was.

As I watched all this unfold from the other side of the street, I held a red ball, common on any playground, to children it was the equivalent of a Swiss Army knife. While she still knelt there in the dirt, that ball slipped from my fingers. It bounced down my driveway, rolled across the street, and somehow managed to stir up the momentum to hop that little curve and come to rest just a few feet from her. She didn't look up, didn't acknowledge the ball at all, and I wasn't about to go chasing after it, I was much too scared for that. In fact I was so scared now that I ran inside the house, back to my soft bed, and back to my window, where I could more safely watch that girl and my ball.

You must understand, I was new to the neighborhood. I had spent the previous six years in Colorado and moved to Southern California only months earlier. My father had come looking for work, so we weren't in the best of homes. Like so many neighborhoods in that part of the state, it was painfully obvious which race lived on which side of the street. My house had a well-trimmed lawn, and while it was not large, it did have a nice flower bed and a short white picket fence surrounding the yard. My house lay on the extreme outer edge of "respectable society," hers did not. It had no fence; the flower bed had been a garden at one point, but now it was barely a compost pile. The tree in the front yard was massive and its roots lifted up the street. The branches seemed to almost fuse in and out of the house itself. There was no garage, only a battered E-Z UP that served as a car park.

However, I remember something very vividly when I first

stepped out of my father's battered Ford Taurus. When I looked at the building I was to live in for the foreseeable future, I thought, *That's a nice house.* And as my eyes moved to the opposite side of the street, *That's an ugly home.* That day, I realized that my second statement might not be correct, but you can be the judge of the covers of books and the labels we do and do not give them.

It was three weeks before the ball moved. In that time there had been plenty of yelling, plenty of fighting, but the ball never moved. I saw the girl looking at it from where I watched from my bedroom window. She was staring at the ball, she must have known where it came from, but she looked at it with the eye of a detective examining a chalk outline. She watched it for a good ten minutes, it got so that I half-expected the ball to roll into her hands of its own accord, or simply burst under that persistent gaze. Neither happened. Instead, she picked it up and looked up at my house and saw me, even as I sat peeking through the shades. Her feet went right up to the edge of the street, paused, and then continued to the sidewalk on my side. She was heading straight for my door. I made sure to get to the knob ahead of my parents and I opened it before she knocked. Her fist was raised, but she lowered it slowly and looked at me.

"Is this yours?" she asked, her eyes not leaving mine. I did not have the same constitution of gaze and so my eyes locked on that red rubber ball.

"Yes, yes it is. Thanks for bringing it back." My hands reached out to take it but she stepped back.

"What's your name?" she asked, her voice losing some of its edge.

"Daniel. What's yours?"

"You have a nice name . . ." She said it with a smile. "Do you want to play?" I hadn't really looked at her up until this point, but her question almost made me forget her lack of a response to mine. I gazed down at her face and realized that she was quite a pretty girl, but it was a fleeting thought as the chance to play with someone my age, in a neighborhood where I knew no one, overtook me. I nodded and there began a two-hour handball game and the closest friendship I ever had.

She never did tell me her name, but I found out nonetheless two weeks later. We were climbing the tree in my front yard, teas-

ing each other about who could get higher. I was trying not to
look down as she called out to me from above, when the front
door to her house was thrown open. I nearly fell out of the tree,
it was so loud. Her father came out in a roar.

"Lucia! What the hell are you doing in that tree! Get your ass
home right now! Your mother needs help with the chores." She
didn't object, didn't say anything, actually, but I saw her hands
tighten around the tree branch, her knuckles white.

Those knuckles were white again five years later when her
mother died. She had slit her wrists in the bathtub. Lucia had
found her there, her mother had a broken arm and bruises all
over her body, it was the sight of a woman with nothing more to
give. I think it might have been easier for Lucia if her mother
was as brutal as her father; it would have made the years that followed so much simpler. As it was, Lucia's knuckles were white all
the more often.

In school she never spoke, she never let anyone talk to her or
touch her but me. Of course at her house she didn't have much
choice, her father could do whatever he wanted, and he did.

The first time I saw her with a broken arm it was her four-
teenth birthday. We had saved up our spare change and we were
going to the drive-in to see *The Dark Knight,* they were going to
play the first and second one together and we both loved Bat-
man. Instead I walked with her for five miles to the hospital, I
held her hand while they moved the bones back into place and
those knuckles turned white again. It was only then, as she held
my hand, that I understood just how tight that grip of hers was.
Like a steel vise it was.

The next time her arm was broken I didn't find out until much
later. She hadn't gone to the hospital, and instead she tried to set
it herself, but she had done it wrong. So I made the walk with her
all over again and watched those knuckles all over again, but this
time she didn't let me hold her hand.

By the third time she knew how to set the bone properly, she
knew how to stitch up a cut too. But perhaps the skill she per-
fected the best was one of makeup, her black eyes and bruises
never showed, she did a good job of that.

Meanwhile I was taking honors and AP classes, we were deep
into high school now and hung out mostly on weekends, I saw
her less and less as I saw more and more of the walls of a class-

room, they reminded me a lot of the walls of my house. The same white paint, the same dull brown doors. My life with Lucia was kept very separate from my life at school, but one was rapidly taking over the other.

At the end of sophomore year I barely spoke with Lucia. We would smile at each other if we passed in the hallways or even across the street, but I was always going somewhere and she was always leaving somewhere else. Every time I saw her I looked straight through the makeup, and I started to not like what I saw. Looking back, I don't think she had changed, not really. But I had, and I was the important one, right?

During the summer of that year, Lucia was caught shoplifting and went to juvie for a month. When she got out it was barely a day before her arm was broken and a deep cut lined her jaw. I thought about offering to walk her to the hospital, but I was working a summer job and she knew how to set it anyway; what could I do?

Then, a week before school started I found myself walking home late from work. I was counting my tips as I went along and looked up to find Lucia sitting on the ground in front of her house. She was fiddling with something in her hands, her fingers seemed to mimic the motions I made just moments before, the bills still parted between my thumb and forefinger.

It was almost nine and the street was dark and deserted. As I got closer I could see what she was doing by the light of a flickering streetlight.

She was holding a rope, one end was thrown up over one of the thicker branches of the great tree that towered over her dirt yard. This was one of the branches that melded into the roof of the house. The other end of the rope was what she was holding, her nimble fingers moving the rope over and over itself. She moved with a precision that said that it couldn't have been her first time. Now, I don't know much about knots, but I know a noose when I see one. She finished the final wrap and pulled the loop tight, her knuckles turning white as her fists clenched the rope.

What I did next was far less wise than letting that ball roll across the street. I yelled, I begged, I tore the rope from the tree and shook her, as if I could make all that pain leave her through sheer vibration. She didn't speak, didn't even notice my presence, really. Then, when I was all out of pleas, all out of words, she simply got up and went inside the house, leaving the noose in my hands.

The next morning I awoke to find a black Lexus parked across the street. I watched through my blinds as Lucia brought out a few bags of belongings and put them in the car. And with every suitcase that came out I saw those knuckles gripping the handle just as tight as could be. The car drove off and with it, Lucia. I didn't see her again until school started, she had been taken by social services and placed in an orphanage. I looked to see if this might help things, return her to the girl I knew, but I didn't understand that she had never changed, not really.

When school began again things were just as they were, except for two rather glaring differences. The bruises, breaks, and cuts were gone, true, but something else replaced them. As all that hurt healed on her skin it seemed simply to sink into her soul. That's what I saw in her eyes, but by now, I didn't know her. We had grown apart in all those years, and soon those occasional smiles as our paths crossed became one-sided, and soon they faded all together.

I was walking home one afternoon in March of our senior year when I saw police cars and tape blocking off my street. I was surprised but not worried; most of the houses on the street had been broken into at one time or another and I assumed it was just another one. I walked up to one of the officers and said I lived a few houses down and needed to get home. Rather than answer my question he asked if I was Daniel Shettler. I told him I was and he immediately led me over to one of the other officers. They exchanged words out of earshot and I began to get a cold feeling in my chest.

Had my house been robbed? Were my parents okay? These and a thousand other worries over my family and house raced through my mind as the men spoke. Then the police officer turned to me and said, "Son, I'm going to need you and your parents to come with me back to the station, I have some questions I need to ask you."

Thus began a three-week investigation. That first night, I was questioned for more than an hour about my relationship with Lucia and her behavior. When I finally went home I saw on the news what had happened. Lucia's father had been found stabbed to death in his house. I didn't realize it at the time, but the previous day was Lucia's eighteenth birthday and, due to her previous record in juvie, she had been released from the foster house.

After all those years of separation I still had some loyalty to her, so when I saw her two months later in a sterile white courtroom, I did find the decency to defend her. In the end she was convicted of voluntary manslaughter and sentenced to five years in a private prison in Nevada. I can't remember her face during the trial, maybe that's because I didn't have the courage to look her in the eye. Even as I defended her character, saying things I wasn't sure I believed, I couldn't look her in the eye. Instead my eyes were drawn to something else, those cuffed hands of hers, with the knuckles white and split, blood leaking out ever so slowly and casting a stark streak of color on those clenched fists.

The memory is a fragile thing and without reminding it tends to forget. So it was with Lucia. She was too far to visit, that's what I always told myself. Yet if I wouldn't walk across the street to see her, no drive would be any different. So my life rolled on, utterly uneventful as high school came and went. I attended Stanford and got a degree in business. Those five years passed without me ever realizing the significance of the number, and when they were up I found myself living alone in a small apartment in downtown LA. The downtown was the only desirable part, I actually lived in what most people would describe as a rather small dorm room, in fact it was half the size of my room at Stanford. Plus it was down the street from the building in which I was an intern, and since my boss knew this, I was constantly being called upon. I had just gotten a text to come in when there was a knock on the door. I began running through which excuses I had already given to the landlord but these all melted on my tongue when I opened the door.

Lucia had always been beautiful, even in a cast she could turn plenty of heads. But this was a kind of piranha gaze that many girls get for features other than their face, because she never smiled much. Even so, I was only ever drawn to her eyes, they always glowed with whatever emotion she was feeling and I had learned to read them like a mood ring. Now, though, I couldn't see anything. She looked up at me, then down at my suit and tie and finally at my shoes, obviously worn but well polished. It was to them that she addressed her statement.

"I'm sorry, I shouldn't have come here, you obviously have . . ." And before I got a chance to speak, think, or even fully grasp her presence in front of me, she was gone. She ran down the hall, something slipping from her fingers as she did. It was a crumpled-up piece of paper, a little wrinkled red ball on the floor. On it was my name and address written in lovely script, not Lucia's. It must have been how she found me. The ball was wrapped up quite a bit and it was clear she must have squeezed it very tightly indeed.

I thought about chasing after her, about taking her to dinner and explaining how sorry I was, but my phone beeped again and I knew I had to go into work. So I made the worst decision of my life, one in a long line, I think.

Two weeks after that there came another knock on my door, my heart lifted, I had been looking for Lucia every night since I last saw her, so I threw open the door. It wasn't her, it was a young man in his early twenties, dressed in what an optimistic observer might call business casual. He looked me dead in the eyes and said, "Are you hurting inside? Are you looking for answers for everything that's messed up in the world? Are you tired of the pain and suffering around you? I can offer you an answer, something more. I belong to a group called the Children of the Dawn, and we believe in a new day—" He was cut off with me slamming the door in his face; after all, wouldn't you do the same?

I didn't think much of it at the time but a few months later I saw a commercial for their "religion" on TV, evidently they had evolved from a "group." It seemed like they offered the universal hogwash that such things are known for, I half-expected them to offer free Kool-Aid at the end with a cheery, "But wait, there's more!"

I had lost my tolerance for such things and decided to go out and look for Lucia again. You must understand that when I said downtown, it was a minor exaggeration. I lived one street over from the outer rim of downtown, but I still called it that since my side of the street faced the backs of those massive monoliths. However, behind my apartment, society digressed quite rapidly, and a line of abandoned warehouses lined the alley behind my building. They were drug-infested holes, as you might expect, and I was always sure to carry a pocket knife when going there. I assumed that Lucia would be living on the streets, so here was as good a place to look as any.

I walked for several hours, inspecting each warehouse carefully before moving on. I was hassled a few times but I was wearing ratty clothes and the only thing on me was my pocket knife. I eventually walked up on a group of homeless men and women huddled around a fire burning in a trash can. Opposite them was a miniature stage. A man stood on it, speaking to them.

". . . but we aren't just about giving you a home and community. No, we offer so much more. We offer a new life, one that frees you from the one thing that keeps all of you here, living like this. Pain. We offer you a cure from pain. This little black pill that I have with me tonight will take away pain, in all forms, both physical and mental. It lets me leave my old painful life behind me and start a new life, full of hope, as a Child of the Dawn." He drew out a small black pill with a theatrical flourish that suggested he likened the action to turning water into wine. The people surrounding him let out a strangely synchronized gasp and the man threw the pill into the back of his throat and closed his eyes. When he opened them again the pupils of his eyes were smaller and the whites far larger. He took out a knife from his pocket and flicked open the blade. Then he slowly dragged it across the underside of his arm. No cry left his lips, no tear graced his cheek, no sign of anything whatsoever came from him. The audience gasped again and then they rushed forward, hands outstretched to take this wonderful gift. Dutifully he began handing out the pills, one to each person, saying, "Join the Children of the Dawn, you can find a new life at the ranch." Each pill was accompanied by a large business card. On it was a picture of an immaculate valley with a large white ranch house in the center; the card read, JOIN THE CHILDREN OF THE DAWN, and an address was printed on the back.

I did not reach out to take the pill or the card, but both were thrust into my hands anyway. Soon enough I was back in my apartment, staring at them on my desk. Some part of me knew what I would find at that ranch, not a new life but part of an old one, one I needed to find. So I grabbed the card and that red crumpled-up paper and started what would be the longest hour-drive of my life.

It was morning when I reached the outer gates; they were opened by a young woman who did not question my entrance. What I saw around me was a world that one could find only in the pages of books. It seemed to be the very definition of idyllic, a little private valley with perfect gardens and great big oak trees. People everywhere all wearing white clothes, and all laughing and talking with such carefree abandon. I was stopped by a woman who gestured for me to park in front of the huge white ranch house. When I got out of the car, she said, "Welcome to the ranch, here is your guide, she will show you what a new life has to offer."

She stepped aside and another woman stepped forward, one with the face of an angel and features I knew but did not recognize. She was clearly Lucia, but not as I had ever seen her. She seemed to almost glow with happiness and a smile stretched her cheeks in a way that seemed almost satirical when compared to her usual expression. But the most disturbing thing was her eyes, they were that full white that I had seen in the young man just a few hours earlier. I could always tell her mood by those eyes, but now I saw only white, nothing of the girl I knew, or even of the woman I'd crossed paths with so briefly. She stretched out her hand and said, "You deserve a new beginning, so let me—"

"Lucia!" I practically wept as I called her name; she did not seem to know me, her face revealed nothing but surprise, and her eyes still less. "Lucia don't you know me, it-it's Daniel, your friend . . . Lucia don't you know it's me?" But the only response I received was her stepping back from me, concern glimmering on her face, but only in the faintest of ways.

So I did all I could think to, all I knew how to. I opened up my hand to reveal the little red ball of paper. It rolled out of my palm and down my fingers, slipping off them and landing on the gravel path. Lucia's gaze followed its every movement, her eyes never changed, but her hands did. Her fingers slowly closed into fists, each finger tucking into place, and then she squeezed, the knuckles turning the same pale white as the building we stood in front of. Her eyes lost that white quality and instead they took on fear, anger, and distress.

I started to speak, but she turned and ran into the house. I went to follow her, but the first woman stopped me and practically dragged me back to my car and sent me back home, to my little apartment at the edge of downtown. I was not to return, since I had "disturbed the peace." A week later I received a letter. It stated, very simply, that Lucia had died of an overdose from an unknown drug, and closed with the barest of condolences from the city coroner's office. Her will instructed that I receive any belongings of hers and handle her funeral. So today I stood alone while a priest spoke of how death was only a beginning. It didn't feel like one, just an end, that came all too soon.

So we return to me kneeling at her grave, my tears are dry now. The act of remembering all that life seems to have dulled death, at least for a little while. I raise my head and look at the headstone one last time. My eyes fall on the epitaph engraved on the bottom. I had it put there as a last-minute addition.

In the week preceding the funeral I had been looking through a box of Lucia's old belongings. I found a book that I remember her often examining. It was called *101 Inspirational Latin Phrases*. It wasn't the kind of thing I expected her to have, and I can't imagine her attraction to a dead language. As I flipped through it I noticed some passages were highlighted and circled; she must have liked those. But there was one I found that she had whited out. Purely out of curiosity I'd scraped away the whiteout to reveal the words now engraved on her tombstone. She might not have appreciated them in life, but in death they were the only words I could find to describe her.

They read, OMNIUM RERUM FINIS ETIAM DOLORIS . . . Everything has its purpose, even pain.

Squish

Squish.

A life just ended. A light has gone out, and not one soul flinched. Three more lights, snuffed, within thirty seconds. They're scurrying about, following their instincts, when a looming shadow is suddenly upon them. Faster they go, trying to evade the inevitable, but—

Squish.

Legs broken, exoskeleton crushed, antennae bent, and with one final twitch, the ant is no more. The weapon of mass destruction used to wreak havoc among the colonies is the foot of a six-year-old boy. A mop of chestnut hair falls over his eyes; he smiles with elation as he plays.

To him, it's just a game.

They're simply ants. They don't mean anything.

Squish.

One final leg twitches.

Her eyes shine as they walk through the halls. His arm around her shoulders, showing the world that they are together. For two years she had been stealing glances full of longing at the boy who spent his springs playing baseball and autumns competing in soccer. A surge of courage during the beginning of her junior year allowed her to shoot him a smile, which was returned.

Smiles turned to waves and waves spun into hellos. Soon he had taken her to the movies, where she had held hands with a boy for the first time. Things were pleasant as she set her sights on New York University; acceptance to her school of choice would convince her that the universe was on her side.

They were growing up, things getting more real. She wants her relationship with him to grow deeper—reach new emotional levels. She utters the truth three weeks before the end of their junior year.

"I love you."

He breaks it off the next day.

He didn't stick around to see the tears begin to drip down her face. They were teenagers—the Youth of America—why ruin that time of their lives with feelings that forced them to stay in one place?

He liked her, for sure.

Lainie was a catch, but she wanted something more than he felt comfortable giving at age seventeen. And it wasn't as if she wouldn't get over it and be dating someone new within the week. This was high school, after all.

As he opens the front door to his house, after coming home from hanging out with his friends, he's not surprised to see his father's car missing from the driveway.

It's not important.

Pushing away the looming shadow over his thoughts, he flops down on the couch, discarding his schoolwork, and turns on the TV.

Fingers tap on a keyboard at an increasingly rapid rate, errors becoming more commonplace—not that the man cared. He was running on coffee, deadlines, and the fear of losing his job. Very few people remained in the newspaper firm.

The lights are dim.

Computers turned off.

The boss tells his employees to head home, but the man remains, determined to finish his article on the new bill passed concerning local teachers' retirement and its effects on the education system. In the back of his mind, a voice tells him to clock out and make it home in time for dinner with his wife and son.

His fingers hesitate for a moment before going back and typing once more. If he doesn't complete this article by midnight

at a level of high quality, the next place he might find himself is
the unemployment line. His eyes flit to the phone sitting to his
right, buzzing as it rings, his wife's name lighting up the screen.
He doesn't answer. Too much work.

He knows the home he'll return to won't be a happy one.
His wife will act like nothing's wrong, though her actions will
say otherwise. His son will be up in his room, claiming to be doing homework when asked to come downstairs. The man runs
a hand through his salt-and-pepper hair as a sigh escapes his
chapped lips.

He's trying; really, he is.

The man loves his family, but the overtime is what allows them
to stay where they are. Times might be tough for them, but he
knows his family has to understand and possesses the strength to
pull through.

They have to.

She looks over at the clock for the fifth time that hour: 9:36 p.m.

She was alone again. The woman rests her head in her hands,
elbows leaning on the dining room table in front of her. The silence of the house became the loudest thing she has ever heard.
Her son was upstairs, but it still felt empty. Everyone was going
about their separate lives, and just so happening to live under
the same roof.

Standing up, she moves to the counter with the intention of
making herself a cup of tea in an attempt to relax. The stillness
of the surrounding atmosphere was unnerving. The vacancy
of each room strengthens her craving for someone to be next
to her.

One would think a mother could turn to her son, but the distance between them was ever growing. The more she urged him
to focus on his studies and make something of his life, the more
he insisted he just wanted to be a teenager.

That everything was okay.

That he was young with no need to worry.

Which, in turn, only caused her to worry more. Her lips go
to the mug in her hands, the soft steam of the tea warming her
nose. Herbal flavors mixed with cinnamon and orange dance on
her taste buds as the liquid spills down her throat, warming her

core. Her eyes flicker to her phone as she sees its screen light up the dim room; there is a text message from someone the voice in the back of her head tells her to stop talking to.

Setting down the mug, she picks up the phone to examine the message. It's a response to a question she had asked earlier in the day when they were speaking face-to-face. The someone had recently become a regular customer at the diner she had been waitressing at for twenty years. Conversations began as small talk while taking his orders, which turned into her joining him during her break, and soon the two were meeting up for coffee when she was off work.

He listened to her. Cared for her. Made her feel wanted again.

She honestly felt that he understood her when she would speak of the regrets she had from never attending university; her hidden desires to do more with the mind she knew she had. His hand would envelop hers, and everything would seem alright again.

He said she was beautiful, that every line on her face was just another part of how she became who she is today.

Fingers tap at the screen, responding to the answer he had given. And, under the assumption that her son was asleep, she slips out the door.

Rays of sunshine stream through the windows of the school, tempting the teenagers with the wonderful weather they would experience after they end their final day. Most of the students hold light hearts with the anticipation of getting another three months of freedom, except for the girl whose heart beats with adrenaline at the thought of what she is about to do.

The final three weeks of her junior year have been anything but pleasant, tears and profanities both being spilled on a regular basis. Questions still racing through her mind, ranging from frustrated to irritated to confused to hurt.

As soon as the final bell rings, releasing the horde of hormonal beasts from their cages, she makes it her mission to locate her target. In under thirty seconds, her eyes lock on to his familiar chestnut mop. He turns to face her when a friend points out the blonde making a beeline straight for him.

Slipping his hands into the pockets of his jean shorts, he attempts to seem collected and casual, when in reality he's dreading what's about to come. It didn't come as a surprise that she was going to beg for him back—they had been good together —but he has to make her understand that things weren't going to work out.

"Why?"

The simple question catches him off-guard. He blinks, not knowing how to answer from off the top of his head. A clap on the shoulder from his friend signifies a wish of good luck before he's left alone with the girl.

She asks it again. "Why?"

Reasons begin to flood into his brain, despite his efforts to push them back. He swallows. "I told you why, three weeks ago."

"No, you told me that you didn't want things the same way I wanted them. You didn't tell me why you felt that way."

He remains silent. She doesn't.

"I loved you, Jeremy. Heck, I still do. That isn't why I'm here, though. I'm here for an answer about why you don't care. Why don't you care about me? Why were we together if you don't care about me?"

It takes him a moment to utter the quiet words, "I did. I do."

"Then why end things?"

"I don't care about you as deeply as you do about me. I probably could, over time, but that isn't what I want."

"Why?"

The question rings throughout his mind, stirring up thoughts and emotions he has done so much to keep under wraps. He stares at the girl in front of him, who is desperate for some kind of closure. Closure he knows he can't give her. Taking a deep breath, he starts to turn to walk away, but not before giving her the simplest answer he can:

"It just isn't, Lainie."

A door opens, and shuts with a bang. Heavy footsteps clomp through the house, and a tired body slumps in a dining room chair. A head pops in from the living room; her apron is still wrapped around her waist from work, an exhausted look in her eyes.

Her husband was never home this early these days. Tentatively, she steps into the dining room, unsure of whether she wants to hear what's going through his mind.

"You're home early." Her voice is quiet.

The man looks up at his wife, the woman whom he has been in love with for as long as he can recall. The woman who, at the mere thought of her, kept him going in the roughest of times. The woman whom he was not pleased to see.

"I'm going to be home for a while now."

He allows the statement to linger in the air, for the realization to sink into his wife's mind. Her face falls further than he thought possible as she slowly lowers herself into the chair next to him. She watches her husband, waiting to see if he will say any more, but no words are uttered. Eyes glancing over his being, she takes account of how he is slumped over, shoulders tense and elbows on the table; his brow is furrowed and mouth set into a deep frown. Part of her says that he is visibly upset due to the current situation, while the other points out that he also didn't look very delighted to see her.

The woman chooses her next words carefully, not wanting the tension to explode. "How are you handling it, James?"

His hard gaze burns into her. "As well as to be expected. It doesn't help that this house isn't exactly a place I wanted to come back to."

Her defenses rising, she snaps, "And why not?"

"I think you know precisely why, Annie." An accusatory tone weaves throughout his reply.

She begins to recount the increasing questions her husband has been having about her whereabouts and the fact that during the past week, he hasn't been calling to check in on her at lunch like he normally does. Her eyes drift away from him, unable to create a legitimate excuse for her own actions.

He sits up straighter in his chair, voice rising. "You aren't even going to deny it?"

Her tired eyes travel back to him. "And how would lying help the situation?"

She sees her husband visibly reel back from her words, stunned that not only were his accusations confirmed but that his wife didn't seem to care. His heart clenches, a whirlwind of emotions racing through him—betrayal fills his chest, anger blinds his eyes, confusion grips his brain, and disbelief shakes his soul. Breathing becomes deeper as he attempts to calm himself down, but as his mind works through the information he has just gained, the harder that becomes.

The whirlwind settles down to just one glaring feeling: pure rage.

Shooting up from his seat, his eyes bore down on his wife, his body seething with anger. She glances up at him with empty eyes, knowing and ready for what was about to come—which just makes his infuriation increase.

His voice echoes throughout the house as he speaks to the woman he married. "You are tearing this family apart!"

This denunciation doesn't sit well with her, causing her placid expression to be replaced with one of disbelief. She stands up to challenge her husband's stance. "Me?! At least I've been home every night, trying to spend time with our son!"

"And how is that turning out for you? He never comes out of his room, and I've been working so late so that he has a room to stay in!"

The discourse continues, insults being thrown back and forth in an attempt to disarm the opponent. Unbeknownst to either, the youngest member of the small family sits on the flight of stairs just outside of the dining room, listening to the result of the tension reaching its boiling point. His mind is still flipping through the real answers to the question he had been asked earlier in the day.

Why?

This is why.

The shouting begins to numb his mind to the point that he can no longer hear his own thoughts. Standing up from his place on the stairs, he takes silent steps past the dining room, past the kitchen, and out the front door.

A layer of gray clouds coats the dark sky, blocking the limited stars he can see on a good night. The air is warm and humid, causing sweat droplets to form on his back. He has been walking for over ten blocks, not caring how far he goes from home.

He wants to get as far away from home as possible.

The stillness of the night helps to calm his nerves and allows him to understand his thoughts more clearly.

Why?

Because he hates the feeling the unknown gives him. Because he doesn't understand anything and yet he understands more than he thinks. Because he wants to talk but he doesn't know who to talk to.

Because he doesn't know the point.

A feeling builds in his chest that he is unable to describe. All he knows is that it feels like he has fallen down a gaping hole with no bottom in sight. His head hangs, the path in front of him lit only by the dim amber glow of the streetlamps.

His eyes watch the sidewalk in front of him, taking note of every crack, leaf, stone, and blade of grass attempting to poke through. His footsteps come to a halt when he catches sight of a small black dot walking about a foot in front of him.

The minuscule black ant scurries along the hard surface, doing its best to reach the haven of the green jungle just ahead. Six little legs are moving quickly, avoiding the sticks and climbing over the small grooves in the pavement.

The boy watches as the ant gets halfway to its destination. It is so small; harmless, really.

He raises up a foot, allowing it to hover over the tiny ebony creature before stepping over it, and both are able to continue on their way.

This time, there is no *squish*.

VICTORIA RICHARDSON

Black and White

Birmingham, Alabama, 1956

I ALWAYS LIKED TO think stepping off the bus was *the* beginning to my summer. I could almost smell the honeysuckle outside Auntie May's home when I stepped off that bus. Summers at
Auntie May's had started after my mother died when I was five,
and I was in no hurry to change it. I had no way to know that this
summer was about to change my life—whether I was ready for it
or not.

"Auntie May!" I threw my arms around my aunt's neck and
pulled her tight.

"Lottie! How are you, darlin'?" She pulled me even closer.

"Doin' just fine, Auntie! Duke! How are you?" My fourteen-
year-old cousin, whose age showed in his attitude, stiffened when
I gave him a hug.

"Lottie."

I laughed. "I'm so excited to see everyone, Auntie!"

Auntie May smiled. "And they're all excited to see you! And
your welcome party will be tomorrow night. I thought you'd like
to rest tonight."

In silence, Duke took my suitcase as his slouched figure walked
to the car.

"How was your school year, darlin'?"

My grin faded before I could freeze it in place. "It was fine,
Auntie." I glanced over at Duke, hoping for a subject change.
"Duke, you've gotten so tall! You're taller than me now!"

He straightened and turned. "I'm almost as tall as my dad now."

We settled into the car and Auntie took the wheel. "Honey, I invited Ruth and Beau over for dinner tonight. I thought you three might like to catch up."

I turned my head to the open window and breathed in the sweet summer air as I grinned. This summer was going to be perfect.

"Lottie!" Ruthie flung her arms in a welcoming hug.

I squealed and hugged my best friend before turning to Beau, who twirled me around. He put me down and I tried to imprint the memory of his scent and his strong arms holding me.

Ruthie cleared her throat. "Do I need to leave?" Her eyes twinkled.

I blushed. "No." Beau threaded his fingers through mine and we all walked out to the backyard. Ruthie and I sat on the swings leftover from Duke's early childhood while Beau leaned against the set.

"So, how have you been? The last time we talked you were stressing about finals." Ruthie squinted against the sun, her freckled nose wrinkled.

"I've been okay." I glanced at Beau. "Daddy was working a lot this year, so we didn't get to spend as much time together as we usually do. How about y'all? How was your school year?"

Beau grinned. "I made the soccer team."

Ruthie rolled her eyes. "You should see him on the field. He thinks he's the coolest cat there."

I giggled. "And you, Ruthie?"

"Well, I joined the drama club at school, and *golly* you should see the lead in the play. He's *so* dreamy!"

Beau nodded. "Isn't he just *amazing*?"

Ruthie rolled her eyes. "You're just jealous every girl in the school is fawning over *him* instead of *you*."

I glanced at Beau, reminded again of how lucky I was. He noticed and winked at me. "I've got my favorite girl right here."

I blushed and smiled as Duke walked up. "Mom said to come in for dinner."

Beau slid his hand into mine as we walked into the house. "How was school *really*?" he whispered.

I was caught off-guard. I thought I had masked it so well. "I'll . . . tell you later."

He turned a thoughtful look upon me. "I'll take you up on that."

I rested my head on his shoulder.

"Goodbye, doll." Ruthie gave me a fierce hug. "I'll be over a few hours early so we can get ready together!"

I grinned and hugged her back. "Good night, Ruthie."

"Do you need someone to walk you home?" Beau looked at the darkening sky.

Ruthie gave a carefree laugh. "No, thank you. I know you two want to catch up. I'll see you later."

"If you're sure . . ." Beau wavered.

Ruthie had already walked into the dusky street, as a cheerful whistle escaped her lips.

I turned to Beau. "Thank you for coming tonight."

He chuckled. "You're my girl. Of course I came. Now"—he pulled me to the swing on the porch and I nestled beside him —"you were going to tell me about how school *really* went."

I stared into the sky for a long time. "Don't tell Ruthie?"

"Why?"

"I don't want her to get upset."

He sighed.

I looked at my hand in his, resting on his knee. Smelled the honeysuckle. And blinked back tears. "I'm such a rule follower, you know." I glanced at him through tear-filled eyes. He rubbed my hand with his thumb, sending warmth straight to my stomach. "And my friends . . . Well, I thought they were my friends . . . They're not."

"Did you get blamed for something?" His protective frown brought a smile to my lips.

"No, I didn't. But when I didn't go along with them . . . We're not friends anymore."

"What did they do, Lottie?"

"They cheated on the tests. And when I found out they did it . . . I . . ."

"You told the teachers."

I nodded, my eyes wet with tears. "I wrote an anonymous note

to the teacher. My friends figured it out, and they were furious.
Did I do the wrong thing?"

Beau pressed his cheek against the top of my head. "I think
you did the right thing, baby."

"Some of them had a lot of pressure to get good grades. You
know how some parents are . . . They keep pushing their kids,
even when they give it their best."

"Did they give it their best before they stole the answers?"

"Yes. And they would've gotten good grades!"

"Then you did the right thing, baby."

I pressed my face against his chest. "Thanks, Beau." A shud-
dering sigh escaped my lips.

I opened my eyes to the sun—and Duke. "What are you doing in
here?" I mumbled, turning over.

"I have something I want to show you."

"Duke, I've been to Birmingham every summer since I was
five. What *haven't* I seen?" I opened an eye to watch him, still
squinting against the sun.

"You haven't seen Birmingham like *this!*"

"Where are we going?"

"It's a surprise."

"Duke . . ." the warmth of my bed was keeping me from moving.

"We're leaving in fifteen minutes," he said, and ran out the
door.

The bus stopped, and I squinted against the morning sun. "Well,
Duke, I haven't been *here* before." I watched the people walk in
front of me. "Where *are* we?"

He shrugged.

"Duke?"

He pushed at the small of my back, forcing me off the bus.
His green eyes followed a few girls as they walked past. "Do you
mind if I . . . ?"

"Duke, you can't just leave me." I reached out to grab him in
exasperation.

"Only for a minute."

"Duke!" I almost stomped my foot as if I was four instead of
sixteen.

"I know where you can stay until he comes back."

I turned to see a young boy behind me. "I think I should stay right here."

"Maybe you should move out of the bus stop? The heat is awful here."

"No, thank you. Duke'll be back soon." I stopped the boy. "Where am I?"

"You're in downtown Birmingham."

I blinked. "Oh . . ."

Before I realized what was happening, another boy ran past me and tugged my purse off my arm. I gasped. "Stop!"

I ran after him in a moment of panic before I realized I had gotten myself even more lost. "Help! Thief!"

I saw the little boy up ahead—much too far for me to catch. I slowed and saw him turn his head—maybe to see if his partner in crime was with him, I don't know.

He collided with a young colored man who fell flat on his bottom. Keeping his wits about him, the young man gripped the little boy's arm and refused to let go, grabbing my purse at the same time.

I rushed over.

"Does this belong to you?" He reached out his hand with the purse.

Without thinking, I helped him up before taking my purse. "Yes! Thank you!" I looked at the little boy. "I could turn you in to the police, you know."

The boy's eyes went wide.

"But I won't—this time. If I hear of you doing it again, I will."

He nodded with vehemence.

"You can let him go." I nodded to the young man.

He did so, and the boy disappeared in a split second. I turned to the young man. "Thank you so much. I'm Lottie." I put my hand out for him to shake, and he looked at it before his darker one joined mine.

"Freddy."

"Just Freddy?" I tilted my head, studying his deep brown eyes.

"Just Freddy." His arm was wrapped around his torso.

"Are you hurt?" I leaned forward, but he stepped back.

"I'm fine."

"Well . . . thank you, again." I scrutinized the way he was holding his arm to his stomach.

"You're welcome." He turned and walked away.

"Lottie!" Ruthie tackled me with a bear hug and a laugh bubbled up inside me. She rushed up to my room where we would spend hours talking, I knew. I followed her into my room, where our two dresses for the night were laid out on my bed. After she had twirled around the room, she soon got bored and begged to get to her favorite part—applying makeup for an evening of food, dancing, and visiting with friends.

The next day was one of my favorite kind—I had nothing to do. I stayed in bed reading until lunch, and after that I sat in the sun, swinging. But I was plagued with worry for Freddy.

Finally, I couldn't stand it anymore. I sneaked out of the house and stepped on a bus headed downtown. When I got off the almost-empty bus, I got a sinking feeling in my stomach as I realized I had come down here for nothing—I didn't even know if Freddy was going to be here again. It was when I felt a tug at my purse—which I had wound several times around my wrist—that I stopped brewing over my misfortunes and focused back on reality.

"You!" I gasped, looking at the same little boy I had seen the day before. This time I was quicker than he was, and I grabbed his wrist.

His eyes widened when he realized who I was.

"I told you not to steal ever again!" My eyes narrowed and he stumbled backward—but not out of my grasp.

"I was—"

I decided not to listen to his explanation. "Do you know where to find that boy you ran into? Where he lives?"

He frowned. "Why?"

"Show me where Freddy lives and I won't tell the police." The words popped out of my mouth. He nodded.

He took me to a part of town with what looked like three-room homes with rickety porches and leaky roofs. "He lives . . . here?"

The boy nodded. "Now, don't tell?"

I glanced at him. "Not this time."

He left me at the door. I chewed my lip. I had come all this way, hadn't I? All I had to do was knock on the door. I raised my hand to rap my knuckles on the wood—but the door was pulled open before I could.

"Oh!" I took a step back, my face heating. "Sorry."

Freddy studied me with his dark eyes, his hand resting on the door frame. "What are you doing here?"

Did that mean he remembered me? Do I reintroduce myself? Or should I just tell him? Will he think me odd? My face heated once again as I realized there had been an awkward silence. "I-I came to . . ."

Freddy's penetrating gaze made me very self-aware as I tugged on my skirt.

"To check on you."

When he raised an eyebrow, I blazed on in my explanation. "I thought that your arm might have been injured when that boy ran into you. I wanted to make sure that you . . . were alright." I swallowed and winced when I heard how loud it was.

"Who is it, Freddy?" a female voice called out. My eyebrows rose.

Freddy didn't take his gaze off me as he called back. "A girl I met yesterday."

More often than naught, a boy who studied me for no particular reason scared me beyond belief. The fact that he was colored could've scared me even more, but for some reason . . . It didn't. In some way, it made me feel . . . safer.

"A girl?" The voice came closer. "Why is she standing on the porch? Invite her in!"

Freddy raised his eyebrow again. "Do you *want* to come in?"

I knew I shouldn't. Not only did my aunt not know where I was, Freddy couldn't have been a year older than me. The very idea of me alone with a boy sent Auntie May to near hyperventilation.

"Freddy?" The girl settled a gentle hand on his shoulder, but it was her gaze that caught my eye. She wasn't looking at Freddy, she wasn't looking at me. She was looking ahead, her eyes clouded. A question in my glance, I looked at Freddy, and back at the girl.

Curious, I took a step forward. "I'm . . . Lottie."

The girl grinned. "I'm Sara. If you're sticking out your hand, I apologize, for I don't see it. I lost my eyesight as a little girl."

"Oh, I'm so sorry." My hand pressed itself against my heart.

She smiled. "No need. I've learned to see with all my other senses. Won't you come in?"

I looked at Freddy, who looked like he was covering a smile. Something inside seemed to nudge me toward the door. I nodded, forgetting she couldn't see me. "Of course. Thank you for inviting me."

Freddy held open the door—a courtesy most young men seemed to forget. "Thank you," I murmured. It took a moment for my eyes to adjust so I could take in my surroundings. One big room served as a kitchen and a living room, with doors that led off to two separate rooms.

"Please, sit." Sara patted on the couch beside her. I did, and Freddy went into the kitchen.

"Lemonade?"

"Oh . . . Yes. Please."

Sara turned to me. "How did you meet Freddy?"

Freddy joined us, catching my eye. Something in his look made me hesitate.

"Lottie's purse was stolen, and I retrieved it for her."

Sara unleashed a proud smile. "That sounds like you, Freddy."

We made small talk for a few minutes, before Sara posed a question.

"Are you watching the clock, Freddy?" She reached her hand out to put her glass on the table. I watched, fascinated that she could put it on the table without seeing. I then looked at Freddy.

Freddy smiled at his concerned sister. "I'm watching it, don't worry."

"Where do you work, Freddy?"

"I work at the grocery store."

"He's not telling the whole story." Sara's eyes sparkled, and it caught me off-guard. "He's participating in the bus boycott."

I looked at Freddy. When it became obvious he wasn't going to explain, I spoke up. "Bus boycott?"

Sara nodded with ecstasy. "When Rosa Parks refused to give up her seat last year, the rest of us decided to back her—we're not using the buses right now."

I tilted my head. "You aren't using the bus? How long does it take you to get to work?"

"Half an hour," Freddy said, glancing at Sara.

"The only problem is, Freddy often works the whole day."

"And I hate leaving you alone."

"He's such a good brother, isn't he?" Sara beamed. "You needn't worry, Freddy. You used to be fine when you had to leave me."

"That was before Hanna got married and didn't have time to check on you." Freddy stood, and my lips began to move before my brain could catch up. "Let *me* check in on Sara during the week."

"You?" Freddy's eyebrows had almost disappeared.

"That would be such fun!" Sara begged. "Please?"

"I've got time. My friend Beau has a summer job and Ruthie's taking a class."

Sara stood, her excitement contagious. "Please, Freddy? I get so bored by myself all day."

Freddy shook his head with a chuckle. "You just said you were fine without me."

"Well . . . I need girl time."

Freddy rolled his eyes. "Lottie, you don't have to do this."

I nodded and heard my heart thud. "I don't mind. The weekends are when I can hang out with my friends and you'll be off on the weekends . . . ?"

Freddy nodded.

"I'll check in on you, Sara. Monday. I'll be here around eleven."

Sara reached out and found my hand, giving it a squeeze. "This is so exciting! I love it."

At the time, if you had asked me why I had spoken up to visit Sara, I wouldn't've had an answer. Now I know it was all part of a plan.

A plan to change our lives.

"Sara?" I knocked on the door. "Are you here?"

"Of course!" Sara sang. "Just a minute. Freddy left his things lying in the hallway—he doesn't normally do this, he was just in a—ouch!"

"Sara?" I clutched a fistful of my skirt and realized I had much concern for this girl I barely knew.

"I'm fine," she called, turning the knob on the front door. "Like I said, he was in a hurry. His alarm clock didn't go off at the right time."

"That's too bad," I said with a frown as I stepped into the house.

"Lemonade? Oh, and Freddy helped me bake cookies last night . . . ?"

I grinned. "I would love some cookies—and lemonade sounds great."

Sara grinned right back at me. "I can tell we're going to get along *wonderfully!*"

Over the next several weeks, we did. We had more in common than Ruthie and I. Not that I didn't love Ruthie any less . . . It was more like my heart expanded. Staying with Sara, I learned that their parents had died, and Freddy had taken care of her ever since.

Sometimes I would be there when Freddy came home from work. No matter how hard his day, it was like he dropped his worries outside the door, once confiding in me that Sara had learned to read him like a book. He never wanted to worry her.

One day, I came by and breezed in, not even announcing myself. "Sara, I brought a new book! I thought we could read it —Freddy! What are you doing here?"

Freddy's eyes had a carefree look I had never seen before. "I have the day off—we were going on a picnic. Would you like to come?"

"I would love to!"

Sara emerged from her bedroom and I looped my arm through hers. "Great! It's a bit of a walk, but it's worth it."

We walked for what seemed a very long time. Bugs buzzed around us and sweat trickled down my back. We finally reached a lake, which enticed me with its cool waters. I slid off my shoes and waded in, laughing at Sara's astonishment at the coldness of it.

"Let's eat!"

We turned, and I saw that Freddy had spread out the blanket and taken out the food. "He's got it all set up," I whispered, pulling Sara toward it. "I hope you're hungry. It looks like he could feed an army."

She grinned. "Freddy cooked it all, too."

I sat down and helped Sara situate herself. "Aren't you a good cook," I teased him.

Freddy nodded. "Sara wasn't much of a help."

"How dare you! I was a very big help in the taste-testing department," she retorted.

I laughed. "Can we eat now?"

Freddy nodded, and they both bowed their heads. I followed suit and Freddy spoke a short, thankful prayer. He looked up and fixed a plate for Sara. "The chicken is at twelve o'clock, the corn cob is at three, and the potato salad is at eight."

Freddy handed me a plate, then fixed his own. After we had finished, I helped Freddy pack up the food and asked Sara if she wanted to go wade again. "Oh no," she laughed. "I'm too full. You two go on. I'll stay here."

I looked at Freddy. He nodded, and we both stood, going over to the water. Within a few minutes of wading, I couldn't help but splash some water in Freddy's direction. With a grin he splashed me back, darting to another area of the lake. I laughed and splashed back.

He counterattacked, and it drenched me. I gasped. "Freddy!"

Freddy's rare laugh filled the air—a smile was often the only reward I got. I got closer in order to drench him as much as me, but he moved further down. Before I could stop, I lost my footing and slid right into him, realizing he had led me right into some mud.

"Golly, Lottie," Freddy said as he observed our predicament. I had fallen on top of him, my face landing in the mud. "You're always getting me knocked down."

"Oh, you!" I shoved him, getting him just as muddy as I. He rolled over and sat up, slinging a replica of a snowball—made of mud—right at me. My mouth dropped open and I reached up to smack him, but stopped short.

My skin was no longer white. I stared at my arm, looking at my mud-covered hand. While I wasn't as dark as Freddy, I still wasn't white. I looked into his eyes, my breathing a little more rapid than usual.

"Lottie?" He frowned, showing his concern. "Are you alright?"

I blinked. "Yeah . . . yeah, I'm fine. We should probably get back. Sara can't hear us anymore."

He nodded and helped me up.

"Thanks, Freddy." I smiled and looked at my skin against his. We weren't black and white anymore. Just . . . people.

*

At home, I decided to sneak in the back door. I hoped to rinse off before Auntie May saw me.

"Lottie? Is that you?"

I whirled around to face Auntie May.

"What *happened*?" Her face paled.

"I was with some friends and we . . . uh . . . got in a mud fight."

"Which *friends*?" Her arms crossed and seemed to intimidate me even more.

"Sara and . . . Freddy," I gulped.

Aunt May frowned. "Was Sara present at all times?"

My thoughts flew back to the mud bath, and a few times before that. But we thought of each other as siblings. "Not . . . at all times."

Her wrinkles deepened. "Lottie! You know how I feel about that."

"We didn't do anything wrong," I squeaked out.

"Still, you shouldn't be alone with a boy!"

"Aunt May—"

"Don't you talk back! You've changed this summer. It's because of those kids!"

"It's not!" I cried.

"I forbid you to see them again."

"What?"

"Never. Again."

"Can I at least say goodbye?"

"No!"

I ran up to my room and slammed the door. I had only known them for a short while, but they had been tucked deep into my heart.

If I had known my heart could hurt like this, I doubted I ever would've befriended Freddy and Sara.

I knew I couldn't disobey her, but I saw Freddy again when he came to Aunt May's house to check on me.

"Five minutes." The sentence was punctuated when she shut the door with force.

"Freddy, I feel so awful . . ."

He looked right at me. "I thought you cared about us. Why did you stop coming over?"

"Aunt May . . . didn't like that we had been—"

His eyes hardened. "That we didn't follow the rules? Times are changing. We're not bad people. I wish you would have the guts to come see us. We won't always be defined by our skin color."

I gaped at him. "I am not obeying my aunt because of your skin color!"

Freddy tilted his head. "Seems like it to me." With that, he began to walk away but stopped and turned. My heart jumped. "Goodbye, Lottie."

After this happened, my aunt tried to take my mind off of the loss of my friends. She thought everything had smoothed over between us, but I was still upset. A small part of me wondered if I should be listening to my aunt.

I began to take in more of the world surrounding me. I noticed signs that told who could enter where in restaurants. The not-so-subtle looks people would sometimes get from the opposite race.

I came to the conclusion it didn't matter what color our skin was, but our character—*that* was what made us who we were.

Once I had come to this conclusion, my newfound belief was put to the test by a pounding on the door in the middle of the night.

"Who is it, Duke?" I yawned and stood behind him.

Duke frowned. "It's that colored boy."

I moved past him to see through the window. "Freddy!" I yanked the door open and was greeted by the sight of Freddy, but I felt the blood rush from my face when I saw Freddy holding Sara in his arms. "What's wrong with her?"

"I don't know." His eyes bored into mine. "Please, help us."

I nodded. "Let me get dressed. We can go to the hospital."

I ran up to my room and got dressed. "Let's go." I matched my strides with his, and put my hand to her forehead. "She's burning up."

He nodded. "It's been like this for two days. I don't know what's wrong. Her fever won't go down!" He looked at me. "If she wasn't this bad, I wouldn't've come."

I blinked. "Let's just get her to a hospital."

We reached the hospital and I shoved the door open for Freddy to walk through. A couple walked in right behind us, and

I stopped at the line of people waiting to be seen. I chewed my lip. "Let me take her to the bathroom, to see if I can get her cooled down. You get in line."

He nodded and I took her. She was as light as a feather—she looked it, too. I did my best to get her fever down by patting her with cold water. It did little good, and I finally took her back out. My arms were straining by that time and I was relieved to give her back to Freddy.

"It's almost time. We're going to get called on in a few minutes."

A nurse came up to us. She looked at us, then at the people next to us. "Who came in first?"

I blinked. "I think we came in at the same time."

The man nodded.

The nursed looked at us again. "What's wrong with her?"

"She's burning up. She hasn't eaten anything for two days and hasn't had anything to drink for one," Freddy responded. "Can you help her?"

"And what's wrong with *her*?" The nurse pointed to the couple beside us.

The husband responded. "A cough, really. It's been going on for a week."

She nodded at the couple. "If you'll come with me . . ."

I frowned. "Wait a minute. You're taking them in first?"

The nurse stood still. "Yes."

"Why? We came in at the same time—and Sara is in more need than this woman!"

"I—"

"Is it because they're *black*?" I glared at her.

"Of course not—"

"How dare you discriminate against them! They aren't beneath us! Their blood is the same color as ours. Why don't you judge *them* instead of their *skin color*?" Hands on my hips, I made eye contact with the nurse. "Show us to a room. *Now.*"

With the realization that I had gone on a rant that might have had nothing to do with the problem at hand, I felt my face flush.

The nurse's eyes widened, and a doctor came up behind her with another nurse. "Helen, please show these three to a room. I'll be with them shortly." He turned to the couple. "If you'll go with Bridget, she'll show you to a room as well. Another doctor will be with you soon."

Satisfied and a little shaky in the knees, I followed the doctor to a room, where he did a thorough exam on Sara. He then delivered the happy news that Sara had a common cold—with an uncommon fever. He prescribed some medicine, as well as an overnight stay so they could hydrate her and get her fever down.

He then left, promising to return within the hour.

Freddy glanced over at me. "What made you say all that to the nurse?"

I sighed, rubbing my temples. "Aunt May is a rule follower. I am too. I saw what I could become. And Freddy . . . I don't want to be my aunt. Some rules are meant to be broken. I want to be friends with whomever I want, whatever their race. People should be judged by their character, not their skin color."

"What are you going to do now?"

I laughed. "I have no idea."

Freddy tilted his head. "That's okay. You'll have me. And Sara."

And I did. Beau and Ruthie, too, once they got used to my new beliefs. In fact, Ruthie became a civil rights activist. Beau and I eventually got married. Freddy became a doctor. Sara is now a mother to three sweet children. And I? You could probably say that I no longer see black and white.

I see glorious colors of character.

The Letters

I LET OUT A loaded breath as I blow or, more accurately, attempt to blow a stubborn strand of baby hair out of my face. Maybe next time *certain* brands should include this warning on all the bottles of their "so-called" extra-strength hairspray: HOLDS HAIR IN PLACE FOR UP TO 24 HOURS EXCEPT WHEN IN CONTACT WITH WATER, WIND, OR . . . AIR. The angry letter to the CEO that I've started to mentally write is quickly dissolved as I step out of my beat-up Honda Civic and take one look at my house . . . or what has become of it. The front door is wide open, every single room in the house appears to be lit, and the voices coming from inside are so loud I silently thank God for blessing us with next-door neighbors who were born completely deaf.

Slamming the door, I march inside as I shout, "*Lucus!*" My oldest son at least has the decency to look guilty as he emerges from his room, holding a laptop in one hand and a pair of headphones in the other. "What was my one request of you today?" I all but growl out.

"To keep the house in order," he mutters, glancing down at his feet.

"And?"

"It's not, but . . . Mom—I swear I only had my headphones on for like fifteen minutes!" he exclaims, widening his eyes to feign a look of purity and innocence.

"Don't even give me that right now. I can hear Anna and Jeremiah yelling at each other over the TV remote . . . something neither of them should even be *holding* on a school night! Not to mention, the house, which was spotless this morning, is a complete mess! And I haven't even seen them yet but Nathan and Jacob better not be digging up holes in the backyard in search of 'buried treasure.'"

At that point I don't even know why I bother marching through the living room to peek out into the backyard, because, sure enough, sitting on the ground covered in dirt and germs and everything gross sit my two youngest sons. I throw a glare over my shoulder at Lucus, who flashes a sheepish grin back at me.

"*Boys!*" I shout through the old screen door. If I hadn't been so tired and angry I would have laughed at the way they scrambled to their feet and positioned their bodies in a sad attempt to hide all the large holes and growing mounds of dirt. "We seem to be unclear about rules in this household!" I yell. "How many times have I explicitly told you that digging holes in this backyard *is not allowed*!?"

"We're sorry, Mom," they whisper as they bow their heads.

"Just go take a shower please. Both of you." With a heavy sigh, I push Lucus by the small of his back into the family room, where the twins, Anna and Jeremiah, are now each silently holding a book. They could possibly have passed for reading if their eyes actually moved across the pages . . . and if Jeremiah wasn't holding a book titled *What to Expect When You're Expecting.*

"Just so you geniuses know," I say, addressing the both of them as they pretend to wrap up their last sentences. "In your attempt to pretend like you weren't watching TV, you forgot to actually turn off the TV."

Immediately Anna's neck snaps up to face Jeremiah. "That was your job!"

"No! You said you would do it if I hid the remote!"

"Well, how on earth do you want me to turn a *television* off without the remote?"

"Well maybe if you—"

"Hey!" I yell. "I don't care whose job it was! Twelve years old is more than old enough to follow simple rules—no TV on weeknights! The three of you are grounded for a week and don't even *think* about asking me to let you stay home alone tomorrow!"

Tears of frustration pool in my eyes. Turning away, I quickly head down the hallway and into the bathroom when I see a cream envelope addressed to me sitting under a massive pile of bills on the kitchen counter. I grab it hastily, head to the bedroom, and collapse on the bed with eyes full of tears from the whirlwind of emotions coursing through me. I toss the envelope onto a small corner of my desk, where three others identical to it lay, collecting dust and the occasional strands of hair.

Ten years ago my husband, now ex, Dave, was sent to prison for driving while under the influence of alcohol. He'd had a passenger in the car with him, and while the bastard was able to physically walk away from the wreckage, his friend was not so lucky. She'd been killed on impact; when the car smashed into the metal pole, her head had also collided with it. And if that wasn't enough for one wife to handle, the investigation into the accident had revealed that the man I was married to had been a little too friendly with this one friend in particular. They had been together for three years. Not to mention the minor detail that she was, in fact, a minor.

I had filed for divorce very shortly after the details of the investigation were released. It was the hardest on Lucus, being only seven years old he not only had to deal with his parents separating, but the fact that the man he had loved and looked up to his entire life had taken a life . . . and would be spending a long time behind bars for it. Part of what made it so difficult was that he was old enough to understand exactly what was going on — but too young to understand how to cope with everything. It was a little easier with the twins, because they were only two when it happened — and it wasn't until they were eleven that I told them the truth about why they didn't have a dad. As for Nathan and Jacob, they are actually my biological nephews. Four years ago, when Nathan was two, my sister passed away giving birth to Jacob. The boys know that while I'm not their birth mother, I'm their mother in all the ways that matter. Initially I hadn't wanted to explain the whole father situation to them. But just like my sister, the boys are as intelligent as they are intuitive. So a couple of months ago when they started asking why they didn't have a dad, I had no choice but to call a family meeting and explain it to them.

After Dave's sentencing, the judge had announced that after ten years, if his behavior was clean and he appeared truly remorseful for the mistakes he had made, there was a chance he could be released. The letters from him started coming in about a month ago. I think when he wrote the first one, he knew the chances of him leaving prison were quite high. He hadn't been in any fights with the other inmates, participated in his group therapy, and had his counselor convinced that he was a good man who just made a mistake, one that happened to be extremely costly.

In the first letter he sent, he had tried to explain his side of the story. That he was so sorry that he had hurt our family so badly. That he was so sorry he had cheated, but that he hadn't felt happy in our relationship for a long time. I couldn't blame him there. I hadn't been happy in a while, either, but we never addressed it because my focus had been all on Lucus, and then Anna and Jeremiah. Dave was the type of person to live in denial. Unless there was a problem that slapped him in the face, he would find ways to avoid dealing with it. In his mind, if he never addressed it, he could pretend like it wasn't happening.

He had ended the letter by saying that his lawyers were confident that the judge would be releasing him soon due to good behavior and that he wanted to reconnect. He wrote that while he understood that I might not want to see him, he had a right to see his children, the ones he hadn't seen in ten years.

After Dave got sent away, I never really had time to process everything myself. One hundred percent of my time and energy went to my children. I worked from home, squeezing in time to take them to and from school and to all of their afterschool activities. I don't think the reality of the situation hit me until ten years later, when I got that letter.

I've gotten three more letters from him since then. I haven't opened any of them and a small part of me hopes that if I close my eyes and cross my fingers it will all go away and I won't have to make a decision. I don't want him to walk back into our lives only for him to leave again, or to make another mistake. The kids deserve so much more than that. On the other hand, what if I prevent them from seeing him and he actually has changed for the better? If they ever found out, they would hate me. How do I know if he's changed? How can I tell?

A knock at the door interrupts my torn stream of thoughts. Lucus, Anna, Jeremiah, Nathan, and Jacob poke their heads into the room and the four of them nudge Jeremiah forward.

"Mom . . . can we talk to you about something?" he asks hesitantly.

"Of course, guys, come here." I scoot over and pat my bed, motioning for them to come forward. As they settle in, Lucus looks up at me and says, "I'm sorry about today. I know you trusted us and we messed up."

"It's okay. I was harsh on everyone—I've been extra stressed out lately but that's no excuse. I shouldn't have taken it out on you," I say as I hug them closer to me.

"Does any of it have to do with the letters Dad's been sending you?" Anna blurts out.

"How did you guys know about that?"

"The other day I went to your desk looking for a pen when I found the stack of letters," she admits. "I didn't open them but it probably means that Dad's out of jail, right?"

"He will be. Soon." I hesitate before continuing. "And he wants to see you. The three of you. I wasn't planning on telling you until I had made a decision but maybe I was wrong in trying to make the decision for you. Sometimes I forget how much you guys have grown up that I still try to protect you from everything humanly possible. The truth is the choice is up to you. Do you want your father to be a part of your lives?"

The question hangs in the air, wrapping its weight around us. It feels like it's moments like these that are the defining moments in your life. That simple yes or no that can change the course of your life forever. Put yourself out there and trust that people can change. Sometimes it's moments like these when you need to stop your thoughts, close your eyes, and take a leap of faith.

I smile at them as I watch my family come to a conclusion. And I sit down, grab a pen and a paper, and begin to write a letter.

Sunday

SUNDAYS ARE SUPPOSED to be warm. You're supposed to wake up to sun drifting through the shades and birds chirping outside. You're supposed to lazily shuffle to the kitchen for a cup of coffee. Sundays are not supposed to be like this. The spinning red-and-blue light does not remind me of the sun. The sirens piercing through the cold air are much shriller than the birds. This water I'm supposed to be drinking is not coffee. It's not warming my hands. Why can't I have something to warm my hands? A stiff blanket has been wrapped around my shoulders but it doesn't make me any warmer. There is a fire in front of me burning bright and filling my vision with orange. I start to head toward it, seeking any form of warmth, but someone pulls me back. A man in a mask sits me back down and tells me they'll be out soon. Who are "they"? Who is *he*? He looks at the plastic cup of water in my hands and tells me to drink it. I don't want to but I do it to make him happy; I thought then he would tell me who *they* were. He doesn't.

When I wake up I can tell that I'm moving. The sirens are still there and they aren't getting farther away even though I know I'm moving. I open my eyes wider to look around and now I know why the sirens aren't quieting. I'm in an ambulance. I'm not hurt or sick, just sitting there, watching. I feel as if I'm watching someone's else's life. There's a girl here. Her skin red and peeling, melting almost. The skin of her arm is missing. I can see the bone and I know that I should be repulsed but I'm not. Be-

cause this can't be real. There are a few people gathered around
her trying to patch things up but I don't think it's working.

"Who is she?" I ask one of them.

No response.

"Who is she?" I repeat it a little louder, willing someone to
look at me, to assure me this is real, but no one does.

The sirens stop abruptly and the doors of the ambulance
swing open as everyone rushes to get the girl inside the hospital.
After everyone has left the ambulance a nurse grabs my hand
and helps me down from the vehicle. She guides me to a waiting room where the chairs are stiff and uncomfortable but I sit
down anyway, waiting for someone to please just tell me what's
going on.

It must be hours later when I wake up to a man in a lab coat
putting his hand on my shoulder. I jump back and notice how
sore I am from falling asleep on that chair.

"Christine." He keeps his voice even and calm; I feel like he is
too calm for the situation at hand.

"Who was she?" I don't see the realization I thought would
possess his face. "Who was the girl in the ambulance?"

He sighs and again the realization is missing from his eyes. He
looks upset, still calm, but in his eyes I can see that something is
wrong.

"It was Ally, your sister. We did all we could but she was too far
gone when the ambulance arrived."

The room is spinning and for the first time since I've gotten
here I begin to appreciate the wooden chair I am sitting on for it
is the only thing keeping me stable.

"I know this is a lot to hear but I have some more bad news.
Your mother did not survive."

I can't think straight. If she's gone there's no one to care for
Gavin and me. I'm only sixteen, this is too much. I can't take
care of him by myself. At that moment I become aware I haven't
seen him since Ally and I arrived here.

"Where's Gavin?"

"He's in your mother's room, and your father is on his way."

I think of how Ally looked in the ambulance. At the time I
may not have processed how badly she was hurt but I hope Mom
doesn't look the same. I don't want Gavin to be in her room, to
see her like that. It would be too much for him to have to look at.

I get up even though the room has yet to stop spinning and try to find him despite not even knowing where Mom's room would be but the man grabs my arm again. I think he says something but I'm too busy worrying to listen. He begins to walk me down a hallway and stops as we get to a door with one window on it that has the shades pulled shut.

"You don't have to do this." His voice is still too calm. "You don't need to see her like this, you can remember her as she is."

I want to tell him what Ally looked like in the ambulance, how I didn't even care, she was unrecognizable, and I was numb to the sight of her wounds but I just push past him and walk into the room.

I had prepared myself for the worst but she looks the same, almost more peaceful. Gavin is curled up next to her on the edge of the bed, looking just as peaceful as her, but there is one difference between the two of them that reminds me this is real: his chest rises and falls as he breathes while hers is still.

I don't want to wake him so I sit at a chair by the end of the bed. There's a clipboard hanging off the end of the bed, I pick it up and try to decipher the medical jargon scratched hastily but I can only make out two words—*smoke inhalation.*

Gavin moves around a bit and opens his eyes. He looks at me and smiles. Gavin is nine years old but he never seems to act his age, not in the sense that his behavior is out of place but just that he doesn't understand social cues or figurative language. He likes things to be very literal and that's okay.

"Christine!" He says it a little too loud and for a moment I'm afraid he will wake Mom but I soon remember that won't ever happen.

"Hey, bud, how are you doing?"

"The doctors said I'm very lucky. I came to sleep in your room late last night and they said if I had been in my room I wouldn't have survived the fire." He winks at me, a weird gesture but one that probably seems perfectly appropriate to him.

There's a knock at the door and Dad comes in.

"Sorry it took so long to get here. They said I can take you two back to my apartment when you're ready." He glances at Mom and I can see he will not be taking it as well as Gavin.

After some paperwork we get into his truck and start driving. The sun starts to rise as Gavin falls asleep again in the backseat.

Dad stares out at the road, his eyes glossed over. After driving for a while Gavin wakes up.

"Daddy? Will you and Mommy get back together now?"

He doesn't answer and I don't either but I can see that he's started to cry and soon I am doing the same. Gavin thinks he upset us and starts to cry as well but not for the same reason as Dad and I.

When we arrive at Dad's apartment he removes the clutter off his couch so we can sit down. He goes into his room and suddenly I'm aware of the fact that the world seems more silent than it should be.

Gavin taps me on the shoulder. "Can we play a game?"

His favorite thing about Dad's house is that he has video games, so we slip in a disk and start to play. Gavin seems unfazed by yesterday's events, but I can't even focus enough to know what game we're playing. After Gavin gets mad at me for dying too much in the game, we switch it to one-player mode and I let him play by himself. I don't even know how to play the game; Ally always played with him. She should have lived; I'm no use to him now. My room is on the first floor of our house. A few years ago I had fractured my knee and all my stuff was moved down so I didn't have to go upstairs. We never bothered to move it back up. That may be the only reason I'm here instead of her.

I watch Gavin play for hours until Dad finally emerges out of his room. His face is red and blotchy but all he does is throw me his car keys.

"I don't have anything to give you for breakfast; go to the grocery store."

His words are harsh, but I don't have another option so I get up to go buy some cereal.

When I get back Gavin is still playing that game, and Dad is sitting at the kitchen table with his head in his hands. I make the three of us bowls of cereal and call Gavin to come eat. We eat in silence.

Gavin goes back to his game but soon turns to me to ask why we're not at school.

"Don't worry about it. You can go back soon."

The rest of the day as well as the next morning is uneventful until Dad's cell phone rings.

"What do you mean? No, that can't be possible, you're wrong!"

He's silent for a few minutes, his face getting redder and redder with each passing second. "Okay, thank you."

I look at him, too scared to ask for an explanation.

After a few minutes he quietly says, "They think the cause of the fire was *A-R-S-O-N.*"

Gavin interrupts loudly. "I can spell; what's arson?"

I look at the game he's playing and actually get a chance to focus on it; there's blood on the screen and the game seems more violent than I remember. I don't know anyone who would set our house on fire. Gavin's only nine, and Ally was even younger. Who would do that to children? Dad looks furious; I know that if he ever finds out who did it he'll set them on fire. His dark-brown eyes are filled with hatred and they're staring right at me.

"You did this," he sputters, pointing his finger in my face. "You did this! You set the fire! *You killed her!*"

At this point he's standing in front of me, leaning over me, and I can feel his spit land on my face as he rants on and on. Gavin has started to cry; he doesn't understand and to be honest neither do I. Dad reaches out his hand as if preparing to hit me across the face, but he seems to see Gavin out of the corner of his eye, and he puts his hand down. He stands there breathing heavily for a few moments before locking himself in his room again.

Gavin collapses on top of me, sobbing loudly.

"It's okay, bud; he's just mad. I didn't set the fire, I would never do something like that, you know that."

"How did he know?"

"Know what, bud? I told you, I didn't set the fire."

"He was yelling at *me.*"

Gavin misinterprets a lot of stuff, so I give him time to think, hoping he'll realize Dad was yelling at me and he did nothing wrong but he just sobs even louder.

"I did it, I set the fire. Why did he say I killed her? Who's dead?"

I don't think he understands what arson means, or what it means to start a fire.

"Buddy, Mommy and Ally went somewhere better last night. They can't come back, but they're happy and they miss us." I start to cry but I wipe away my tears because seeing them will only make Gavin more upset. "Do you know what it means to start a fire?"

"Yeah, that's what I did last night. Dad taught me how when we went camping over the summer."

"You set a fire last night?"

"Yeah."

It's becoming too much to process. Why would he even do that? What happens if the police find out? Can they send a nine-year-old to jail? Will they take him away from me? Will they be able to understand him? Will they know that he didn't mean it? I decide to take it one question at a time.

"Why did you set a fire in our house, Gavin?"

"I wanted Mommy and Daddy to live together again. Ms. B said tragedy brings people closer together."

What?!

"I just wanted them to be together again, Christine, please understand."

I want to tell him that I can't, I can't and I won't ever understand but that's not what I tell him.

"Of course, buddy, don't worry, we can fix this."

Dad left his cell phone so I grab it and step outside to redial the last number that called him.

"Hello? This is Christine, Tom's daughter. I was just wondering what you told him about the house fire on Beechwood Street earlier yesterday morning."

"Ma'am, we can't just give out that information."

"Please, I've just lost my sister and my mom; I'm more of a parent to my younger brother than my dad has ever been and I need this information to make an informed decision of what my brother and I need to do next."

There is a sigh that comes from the other side of the phone. "How old are you?"

I know it's wrong but I need answers so I lie and tell him I'm eighteen.

"If it comes down to it are you willing to act as the legal guardian for your brother?"

"Yes, of course."

"The Beechwood Street fire seems to have been caused by arson of a crude nature. Not very professional, probably done by someone with little experience. So far the prime suspects are people who were inside the house at the time of the fire or have access to the house, because there were no signs of forced entry."

"No one has keys to our house if they don't live in it and if Ally and my mom are dead, your prime suspects are . . ."

"You and your brother. Sorry, ma'am, I'm only the messenger, but if anyone calls to ask, you've never heard of me. Good luck, ma'am."

Just like that, he's gone. I slide down against the wall, clutching the phone. I have two options, turn myself in or let them take Gavin away. They can't take him, but if I turn myself in there will be no one to look after him. Dad wasn't a good parent before and now he barely leaves his room. We have no family he could go to, no grandparents or aunts or uncles. I sit there staring blankly for a few minutes and decide that I'll have to choose. Gavin may be literal but I'm rational and I can make this choice. I have to weigh the pros and cons of each option, because no one else is going to do it for me.

If Gavin gets taken away he might end up in juvie. He wouldn't even understand what was going on or why he was there. He also might be admitted to a psychiatric hospital for the criminally insane. With the thought process that led him to do this how could he not be insane? Would they even put him in there, considering he's only nine years old? So far this option only has cons and no pros. I guess if somehow he wasn't charged at least he could still have someone to care for him.

If I turn myself in Gavin could be taken away by Child Protective Services, or even worse he could remain in the care of our dad. There would be no one responsible enough to take care of him and I would be in jail. He wouldn't even understand what had happened. The only possible pro for this yet again would require a miracle. If I wasn't charged for some reason, things might turn out okay.

My list of pros and cons races around my head all night, practically driving me insane. Gavin and I sleep on the couch again.

I spend all of the next two days trying to make a decision. Dad only comes out of his room to eat. He doesn't say a word and refuses to look at me. What would he do if Gavin told him what he had done? I don't even want to imagine it. Late Thursday night I make my decision. I'll have to turn myself in. Maybe Gavin will be adopted by a nice family who understands him. I know that's almost impossible but it's the one thing that keeps me going as I drive all the way to the police station.

I swing open the heavy glass doors and step inside. There's a man in uniform sitting at a desk in front of me. There are plenty of chairs but they're all empty. I clear my throat.

"Hi."

He holds up his finger, asking me to wait a minute. He seems to be scribbling something down on some paperwork. A minute or so later he looks up at me.

"What can I do for you, sweetheart?"

"On Sunday morning there was a fire on Beechwood Street."

He stares at me.

"I did it."

"You did what, honey?"

"I set the fire. It was my house. My name is Christine and I set the fire on Beechwood Street."

He peers over the rims of his glasses at me and gets up with a sigh. He mutters under his breath as he handcuffs me.

"Someone will question you shortly, Miss Christine," he says while guiding me to a room with a table, two chairs, and a mirror. I've watched enough crime TV shows to know that's not really a mirror.

After what seems like hours a woman comes into the room with a file in her hands.

"How old are you, honey?"

I just admitted to setting a fire that killed two people. Why is she calling me "honey"?

"Sixteen."

"You know what I think? I don't think you set the fire, I think you're covering for someone."

My heart starts to race. How could she know? I literally just walked in here. They had two main suspects and one of them just walked in the door and turned themselves in. What could possibly tell her that I didn't do it?

"Umm . . . what?" My voice cracks.

"Only like ten percent of arsonists are female and usually they're setting fires for revenge. Also, nothing about you says arsonist, you're just a normal girl caught in the crossfire as far as we can tell."

Oh, she has no idea.

"Listen, since you turned yourself in we've got to keep you for twenty-four hours. Make yourself comfortable and feel free to use your one phone call."

Defeated, I pick up the phone and dial Dad's cell.

"Hello?"

"It's Christine, can I talk to Gavin please?"

There's a click as he hangs up. Wow, great.

For the second time this week I spend the night sleeping on an uncomfortable chair in a place I don't belong. This time it's made of metal and I wake up even sorer than the last time. I'm brought some food but that's the only outside contact I have until long after the dinner plate has been brought. The woman comes in again.

"Good news and bad news."

"What time is it?"

"About midnight. Do you want the good news or the bad news first?" She tries to say this tauntingly but it comes out more sympathetic than I think she meant it to be.

"Uhh . . . good news?"

"You get to go back home. Bad news is we know who did it and I don't think you're going to like the answer. You called someone here at the station on Tuesday."

Oh no.

"We're not going to talk about the fact that you lied about your age, we're just going to talk about some information that was exchanged over that phone call. You were told that you and your brother were the main suspects in the investigation, correct?" I don't answer her but she continues anyway. "You informed the officer that you wanted to protect your brother, not in those words but more or less, right?" Again I say nothing. "That really only leaves us with one solution."

She looks at me with an attempt at a smirk on her face but her eyes give away her empathy.

We drive over in a cop car and she knocks on the apartment door. Dad opens the door, disgruntled and unshaven.

"What do you want?"

"Is this the home of Christine and Gavin Jensen?"

"It is now." The way he says this reminds me he still thinks the fire was my fault, that I killed Mom on purpose.

Gavin comes running up to the door and the smile is wiped

off his face as he realizes who's there. I start to cry. I wish I could stop it for his sake, but it's all too much. The woman removes my handcuffs and coaxes a sleepy Gavin toward her. She begins to state his rights but he doesn't even understand.

He looks at me with tears streaking his face. "Christine, you said you would fix this, I didn't mean to do it, I don't understand." He chokes the last part out through waves of tears as he is taken away.

Somewhere a clock chimes midnight. It's not warm out, no birds are chirping, there is not a ray of sunlight or a cup of coffee to be seen, but nevertheless, it's Sunday once again.

AMELIA VAN DONSEL

The Flood

THE STOVE WHERE they cooked meat that looked like a cocks-comb was submerged in a turbid pond. The cutting board where they ritualistically sliced ingredients when there was no more canned food to be reheated was lost to the subaquatic world. The carpet had become nothing less than a mushed, unnatural bottom to the river that snaked into closets and restricted rooms. The earrings and pendants Nathan's mom had received for her birthday were rusting beneath the waves in their unopened cases, and Nathan's wildlife adventure books were all but waterlogged in the anomalous aquarium. The pristine water that filled the apartment shimmered in a hot, glinting dawn, like the surface of a planet.

Nathan's mom worked fervently, bandana strapped so her forehead was crested with a folded star, and arms weighted with buckets of water that warped whenever she tried to wade through the pool. There was barking from Stacy, Mr. Reed's schnauzer, and she swished over to shut the window. She wished some of the mothers would help her or maybe find her collapsed in the vast puddle, dead from exhaustion, leaving the water to soak into the bedsheets, the drapes.

God, not the drapes.

She would need bigger buckets.

The damp July had saturated the town's skin with water. Rain had eroded the world's color, leaving it in various stages of gray, and the sun, a vague, dim haze behind the wall of cloud, now sputtered like a dying lightbulb. Sidewalks were slick with tears, clean leaves pebbled with rain were glued to the streets, and there were basements that needed pumping, like a toxic stomach, that week.

But there were puddles to skid through on three wheels, brown murk whose inhabitants were to be sketched colorfully with dulled crayons, soddened grasses to wade through, and soaked playground slides to run up, ones that squealed when rainbow boots, sloshing with water, met plastic. Everything was slowly draining, no longer pouring from roofs in clean sheets and lines, but sliding off of umbrellas in fat beads.

This had caused a minor inconvenience in Apartment Complex 312. Water had flooded the narrow throats of hallways in the basement and the ground floor, gushing over stairwells until you could slide into it like a pool.

Evidence of children floated everywhere. Bath toys, cardboard books, stuffed animals whose polyfill was buoyant enough to keep them aloft, all bobbing down corridors, in dining rooms like the spilled contents of a shipping container. But the six-year-olds loved the clatter the synthetic aggregation made when you waded through it, their noses high, elbows cocked above the water. The eight-year-olds loved slinging their slender legs onto tables, beating their hairless chests with declarations of the Water Kings. The four-year-olds loved being paddled by makeshift canoe through the lobby, rescuing the sunken Slinkies, the floating stuffed dogs and books like tsunami survivors, from the drizzly apartment alleyways.

Nothing worked. The power was shot, the air visibly sizzling above lines of dormant, dysfunctional air conditioners, their polyphonic static hum no longer chugging and sucking away at the collective dust and fuzz and hair of the complex. Everyone longed for that fake cold. Humidity was seeping into the walls, and adults opened windows trying to compensate, instead letting in thick blocks of air. Blinds warped and sagged like jowls, toothbrushes nodded by, plants wilted like the upper-level tenants on the couch.

Adults were on their separate floors, drawing up paint cans of the mysterious liquid and hurling it out the window. The landlord, stuck in traffic somewhere on the I-95, said that he had the industrial pump somewhere in his truck, and that the tenants would have to make do in the meantime. But they didn't mind initially, not caring to admit how cool the muddy water felt against their arms plunging down deep into it. Those old enough to help did, those young enough to drown in the nearly waist-deep water were sent outside to the communal spongy rectangle of grass.

Bathtubs and blow-up pools were mundane if there were a pond in your house with free canoe rides. Happy plastic sandals smacked the sidewalk in protest, windows were pounded on with furious fists; there was profuse wailing. Children each found something to hurl across the yard—rocks, firetrucks, grass, Velcro shoes—with their tiny, sticky hands, each screaming, pleading to someone else inside, *Don't fix it, Don't fix it.*

Eventually the children stood like inmates, bending and straightening their legs, exhausted by the heat and futile clamor, some convicts chubby, some spindly, some old enough to realize that all their things were ruined. Most were sprawled on the soggy ground in the exaggerated despair of childhood, enclosed by a diamond wire fencing their fingers curled through desperately.

Nathan could remember balancing on his toes at the counter of a 1-Stop store (he was still small enough to fit in the best places during hide-and-seek), the woman there finding different reasons to open her mouth.

"Those sunglasses are half-off, dear," she said, rapt, dropping her magazine at the sight of him. Nathan only cared about the revolving stand. There were cards and eye-level candies and pens and flashlight keychains and sodas to play with. The woman put a few more rubber bath toys into his hand before she jumped, remembering something. "I have *just* the thing for you," she squealed. She leaned across the counter again, this time reaching up onto a shelf.

In her arms was an enormous stuffed dog, its floppy ears dragging, its ridiculously shimmery coat outfitted with a bright-blue fake leather strap. Nathan's mom had finished reading the ingredients on the cough syrup bottle and glanced over.

"Isn't he just *fabulous*?" The woman's voice raised in pitch. "And he has a collar and *everything*. I keep him around for kids like you."

Nathan remembered his mom shouting and the dog staring at him and the little tinkling of the bell over the main door.

Nathan shoved his sneaker farther into the mud, releasing water that bubbled up from the earth with a revolting spurting sound. The color reminded him of the dog's fur.

Around the yard, a few toys still lay intact from the harassment earlier, including a few purple hairbands that were twisted in agony yet remained unbroken from window slingshotting. There was a depressive game of pirates he could get in on or maybe the knee-high rock tower, its moat a desperate little sludge ring dug out by the youngest of the bunch. There was all of that, Nathan realized, but there wasn't a limited issue of *I-Rex,* the comic of the cybernetically engineered supercanine, to tear through in the early hours of the morning while cocooned in I-Rex sheets or to flip through over his PB&J lunch as he frantically brushed away sticky crumbs. He imagined his collection rippling at the bottom of his room's new pool. The ink would bleed and run like mascara as he lifts a copy up by one corner, the story line indiscernible, I-Rex's cybersnout fading white into the background. The pages would dampen into fibery mush in his palms or lose their sheen and freeze stiff and wavy, crinkling as he turns them.

A shadow fell over Nathan, grumbling. "I guess we could take hostages or something."

Nathan pulled up his shoe and quickly wiped at his nose. "What?"

"We could take hostages. Like they do in those movies." A short Hispanic boy in an unflattering yellow shirt stood above him, his hands wrapped around a stick he had sharpened via the sidewalk.

"What do you mean?" Nathan asked.

He looked down at it. "So, okay, it's not a gun. But maybe we could point it at someone's neck and give a list of demands. They'd listen to us."

Nathan looked around. There were no immediate volunteers. The boy sat back down.

They could hear the adults arguing in the basement—what would they do about these dryers and why wasn't Brian getting more towels and was this covered by the insurance and where was the landlord at a time like this. You could see their figures,

their curving backs, probably aching from hours of dunking, un-
derarms darkened and damp hair clinging to their faces. They
had tried to explain to the children that the apartment was
like a capsized boat: if they didn't get the water out in time, it
would sink, and they needed complete cooperation. Then they
set them in the yard and said they'd check on them later. One
girl recalled an inducement of ice cream before having the door
slammed behind her.

Finally, in the dusk that dropped behind the soggy town, the
children admitted defeat. They watched water settle in road cra-
ters, thick drops slip down the sides of houses. In puddles, gaso-
line rainbows swirled with a peacock's iridescence. Everything
stuck to everything else, and the dark was becoming difficult to
breathe. What they wanted at that moment, perhaps more than
something to do, was cold, dry air; the kind with a bit of pine in
it that reminded you of fall. It occurred to Nathan that people
could die from this boredom stuff. It happened, surely. Parents,
wanting to be alone, naively believing that imagination would
grab hold of young minds and paint over the muddy landscape
before them with nothing more than fictitious castles and beasts
and spaceships, released their children only to find them strewn
about the yard hours later, dead from acute ennui.

Nathan pushed up his glasses (they were the same blue as I-
Rex's collar, from the rack at CVS) and glanced at the devastated
tenants around him, slouched in corners from the searing heat.
He looked longingly across the street to where Mr. Reed was letting out Stacy. A jogger passed, oblivious to the temperature, and
then a wondrous reprieve from the tedium came into view. Tentatively, as if she might break a heel, a small myopic woman with
a collie the color of dryer lint was wobbling down the sidewalk.
Nathan had seen them in the winter, just two furry figures fighting the inundation of snow like mammoths, like what collected
on their backs and shoulders might bury them as they trudged
steadily forward, chapped faces down. While they were still in-
credibly slow, it was remarkable how much fur they both had
shed.

Their shuffling drew the children from their haziness and to
the chainlink fence. Fifteen pairs of eyes watched in desperation,
and as they neared, small arms outstretched in the metal gaps,
shoving viciously, each hand more eager than the last.

Just as Nathan reached across, straining as far as he could to scratch and to pet a creature that was not the goldfish his mom was always trying to get him to like, the endless guinea pigs, turtles, gerbils that had all inhabited his apartment, had died uncared for in a cardboard box or toilet. Just as he struggled forward, he felt around his wrist all the times his mother's fingers had dug firmly and pulled him away, and it startled him. Jolted him, even, not to have pain in his hand. He had barely grazed the coat, but it was the most wondrous texture—strands of wavy fuzz against his skin, warmer than any stuffed animal.

As the pack of children chased it down the fence, Nathan rolled a clump of fur between his fingers. A quiet girl who was carrying a stuffed cow that had been depressively soddened into an unidentifiable brown mass was suddenly beside him.

"Can I . . . feel it?" she murmured. Tentatively, he handed it to her, and she stroked it, running its sleekness across her palm, studying the thinness of the filaments like it was a feather. Their palms wrapped greedily around each strand, hungry,

Then there was yowling from Stacy. Maybe she was lonely? Maybe the collar Mr. Reed bought for her was too tight? Maybe she needed water for the heat?

Nathan wasn't allowed anywhere near Stacy. Still, they did like her wiry gray coat, her patches of scratchy, sallow skin. They adored the few, always-slightly-damp hairs of her muzzle fuzzed with white. Her sleepy, fourteen-year-old waddle (hip dysplasia, actually, but Mr. Reed's eyesight was going) and her countenance that caused her to yawn, then clamp down with an overbite. Her sour, pale gums and dry, ribbony tongue. Her tufts of withering fur hanging over her drooping, beady eyes that reflected quite freakishly in the dark. Her lumpy, flopped ears, perpetually itchy, that only the strokes of neighborhood children could soothe. Her warped claws that they imagined clicked frenetically on hardwood floors. They fed her like they were feeding a zoo animal, only with Pop-Tarts and rawhide (all too dense for her nine yellow teeth), which required an exclusive trip to Pet-World. They loved pooling their money to buy her an orange bird that sang when you squeezed it or a rubber cube with a rope attached to it, and whenever they came Mr. Reed would open the screen door with an appreciative smile and say, *You come back anytime, now.*

The horde of them looked to Mr. Reed's yard, Stacy's coinlike eyes flat and floating and beckoning in the dark.

It was a night the color of blackberries, a white-hot moon standing above, watching the wide, pale faces of children. The fence was locked, but Nathan, after one more glance to the window, scaled it. *Star Wars* boxers snagging, he made it with a thud on the other side. He fixed his glasses and studied the street before him, his sweaty hand, for the first time, empty of an adult's.

As the adults loosened their clothes, the world seemed to do the same, their figures wavering like mirages in the night's heat. The air had a resilient sizzle, and every surface touched was viscid and warm, nearly malleable. Dirt, woodchips, and grass had been somehow suspended in the undulating pool like bodies swirling in a grubby galaxy.

Nathan's mom pulled up a dripping pair of her son's shorts, which he had experimentally left on his bed covered in butter for three days. She was afraid it would begin to attract wildlife if left unattended. There was enough sweat to cloud her vision, and her body was so shaky and soaked she could barely discern the cold-coffee water from perspiration anymore. It was getting late, and even after hauling for a full day the water had barely begun to lower. She knew the dangers of slowing—the rigorous pumping followed by dampness followed by mold followed by contractors like a pricey fucking remodeling parade.

She felt something shift its weight inside her. Maybe it was the underlying fear that at any moment someone could come into your house and kill you and your child with a chainsaw. Maybe it was how Nathan never looked both ways before he crossed the street or how he always tried to take home a menacing plastic dinosaur or miniature space gun during trips to the dentist. When friends were over, there was no sword fighting, no tribal wars. *It's the principle of it, that's all,* she'd explain to them as she collected plastic sheaths and knives during Nathan's birthdays, although she never really knew what that meant herself. During story hour at the community center, where the carpet was riddled with gum and trails of crackers, Nathan used to cry when she informed him it was time to go, the story was getting too violent. There was never any Hansel and Gretel, Jack and the Beanstalk, to be heard. Nathan's mom recalled the vacant eyes that followed her as she exited each toy store, each movie theater, puppet show. She remembered yanking him away from an employee at the science museum ("Radical Ranger Ruth") who was showing off a lemur. It was something close to safety, but it wasn't safety.

Throughout the day she had heard pitiful sighs and one *How sad* as the young, upper-level tenants observed her from the hallways. *Isn't there someone to help her?* they'd asked each other before turning back upstairs. And then there were those—the older couples, mostly—who'd peered into her apartment to watch her heaving with exhaustion and had derided her with a quiet, *She had it coming, never lets her boy do anything nice.*

She kept pouring and dunking and dousing.

She thought about moving, maybe to someplace cooler, with fewer nosy neighbors and fewer gnashing dogs. Minnesota? She wished she took walks at night to view the soap operas of the neighborhood through their windows. It was the cosmopolitans who did that, she decided. Instead she stayed inside and watched the soap operas on TV. She wished she'd joined a gym, she wished she bought more produce. She wished she had let Nathan have his fucking dog.

And at that she looked to the window for him.

The air was buzzing and bubbling with the night's chatter. A rush of smoky hot air billowed Nathan's T-shirt as cars whirred past, their headlights grazing bushes with ghostly projections of light. It smelled like the town was adapting to the water, the damp air of warping wood and soaked fabric and industrial-strength cleansers. Pine needles washed downtown by rain were spread like orange centipedes beneath Nathan's muddy sneakers. Meanwhile, children were being unloaded from the top of the fence, dropping beside him as he moved to the edge of the pavement. Stacy was alone. Mr. Reed had gone to bed early that night; he'd been feeling ill.

Nathan shifted his feet, his teeth clamping. He missed the warmth, the feeling of heavy fur intertwined with his fingers. He wanted a scratchy tongue against his palm, a chin to knead, a pair of eyes to look back at him and say, *Yes. Yes. Thank you.*

The short crowd stood against the fence, sweating in silence. Nathan saw it like he was I-Rex: deft, elusive, fearless. There was no crosswalk. There was just a moment of emptiness in the street.

And in the split gap between passing cars, slashing metal, Stacy's head lifted as Nathan sprinted off the sidewalk, slipped on the leaves, and skittered onto the asphalt, his glasses flying across the road, so many miles away. Nathan's hands scampered wildly, clawing and groping at the grit for a glasses-like shape as his vision was reduced to slow-motion blurs, like a soddened comic book.

The landlord had gotten off the I-95 and was late; he had promised them the pump by nine. And he was especially anxious to find out if there'd been any damage done to his couch and damn one of his headlights was out and he was checking his watch and comparing it to the one in his truck and wondering why it wasn't the same when he saw something on his right some woman probably that new mother he always did like her looking wide-eyed looking down and he looked to the street where it was too dark to see what she was pointing to.

Contributors' Notes

TAL BAJAROFF is a ninth-grade student at Miami Beach Senior High and lives at home with her family of seven. She enjoys the arts but hasn't really considered herself a writer so much as a singer (so much that she has her own band). She wrote this short story with her stepsister Ella Rabino, who she claims is the only thing—along with the dogs—keeping her sane in a house so full of people.

KAYLA BERNHOESTER is seventeen years old, and she has been writing as long as she can remember. She's an award-winning artist who fell in love with theater, music, and artistic design. She plans to attend Webster University in St. Louis to pursue video game design or acting.

JARYN BLAIR is from Phoenix, Arizona, and is a student at Sandra Day O'Connor High School. She enjoys reading, writing, and drawing. She loves spending time with friends and family and seeing the world's sights and cultures. Jaryn participates in theater and writing club at school. In the future she hopes to pursue her dreams of becoming an author or a physical therapist for animals.

NIKI BORGHEI is passionate about books, literature, philosophy, language, and art. Since fourth grade, she has been in love with reading and writing, which seem like magical tools to create and travel to new worlds. Her favorite things to write are short stories and poetry. Niki also enjoys arts and crafts, including bookbinding and calligraphy. In the future, she hopes to start a business or become an English teacher. Her dream is to continue writing throughout life to inspire people to follow their dreams.

CARLO DI BERNARDO is a junior at Evanston Township High School in Evanston, Illinois. Surprising circumstances brought him to the United States; he used to wake up in a small village in southern Italy. This is why his stories always take an unexpected turn. He loves to create his own music, has a passion for cooking, and cannot stop playing soccer. "The Sickle" is his first published story.

A dedicated student, loving daughter, and friend to all, KYLA DUHART's interests vary. She loves to photograph nature, advance her knowledge in math, and, most importantly, follow the path God has set for her. She is on the honor roll, has received a 4.0 grade point average, and is a six-year attendee of Centerpoint Church in Colton, California. Her future goals include a math profession, continuous attendance at her church, and to be everlasting friends with her best friend, Athena O'lear Thompson.

ADELLE ELSE resides in Alexandria, Virginia. Writing, art, and photography have always been strong passions of hers. In the future, she aspires to travel the world, seeing as many places as she can, seeking to capture them in words, photos, and on canvas. Much of her writing inspiration comes from places she has seen and the nature around us. Some of her favorite places she has visited are Dubai and Hawaii. She has earned a black belt in tae kwon do and is proficient in four languages. She intends to keep writing and see where it takes her in the future.

BETHANY HALL wants to become a high school English teacher. She loves to play piano, which she has been studying for six years.

She is the youngest of six children, and her father is a pastor. She has won two other writing awards from Scholastic.

The author of "Only a Fool Would," AAMNA HAQ is currently a high school senior in California. She loves reading, especially mystery and science fiction novels. She is involved in journalism, creative writing, and STEM, and hopes to be able to pursue work in all of these areas when she is older.

ANNIE HOANG is a fourteen-year-old student from Portland, Oregon. She lives out most of her days enjoying the rain, learning new things, and hanging out with family and friends. Every other moment is spent delving into fictional worlds and inventing her own through her writing. When asked what she wants to do when she's older, her answer is constantly changing, but her goal in life is to make a positive change. She would like to thank you for reading her writing (including this very-awkward-to-write biography), and hopes that her words have given you something to take with you.

MORGAN LEVINE is a poet and junior at the High School for the Performing and Visual Arts in Houston, Texas. She is a two-time finalist for Houston Youth Poet Laureate. When she's not doing homework, she's drinking coffee, playing soccer, or being inspired by her beautiful and strange friends and family. She enjoys comfortable silences, Mark Rothko, and collaborative playlists.

SIMON LIU has always been interested in trying new activities and experiences. He is a member of the Herricks High School student government, treasurer of the garden club, as well as a member of the cross-country team. Currently, he is very interested in learning more about the technology that powers our world as well as taking an active role in his community. He is fascinated by how vast the world is and the infinite possibilities it contains, and his aspiration is to never stop learning and pursuing new ventures.

AELA MORRIS is eighteen years old and a student at Evanston Township High School in Evanston, Illinois. In addition to writing, she enjoys playing the violin, editing her school's literary magazine, and volunteering. She has won several local poetry contests and wrote a monologue that was featured in the Statue Stories Chicago project. Aela's future plans include studying creative writing and history in college.

RUSHALEE NIRODI is currently a senior at Mission San Jose High School. She is an avid reader, and her favorite series include Harry Potter and the Shadowhunter Chronicles, but she is always looking for something new to read. She also loves performing and is currently applying to colleges as a musical theater major. She hopes to continue writing throughout her life and is always excited to start working on something new.

JOSHUA PECK has had a great fascination with audiobooks and has listened to hundreds of books. He started writing seriously in high school and has written a few dozen short stories. While much of his early work is not very good, he believes that even the bad work he has written has taught him something not to do next time. He also enjoys camping and has hiked nearly six hundred miles. He is currently a senior and is looking to pursue a degree in creative writing and earn his teaching credentials in college. He hopes to spend a few years as a high school English teacher and maybe write full time one day.

Storytelling has been an important aspect of HANNAH PERRY's life for as long as she can recall. She keeps a journal and pen with her at all times, and is always turning to new people and experiences for inspiration. During the summer of 2016 she entered and won the high school division of a local essay contest for *Kids' Standard* magazine. She has taken honors English throughout high school and is currently enrolled in AP English as a junior. She enjoys participating in the writing club as well as in forensics —competitive public speaking—and she is one of the captains of her school's team. Hannah hopes to attend a good college and pursue a degree related to writing so that she can include her passion for storytelling in her career.

VICTORIA RICHARDSON is a homeschooled sixteen-year-old and has been writing stories since she was eleven years old. Her favorite things to do include spending time with family and friends, writing stories and reading books, and acting and singing on-stage. She's always been interested in writing, and has lately been looking into becoming a social worker—right now she's waiting to see where God wants her. She's very excited to share her story with you and hopes you enjoy it. *Soli Deo gloria!*

DESTINY TRINH is currently a senior at Kennedy High School in Fremont, California. She is part of many different organizations including DESI (a Bollywood dance group), the Vietnamese Student Association, her school's ASB, and tennis, for which she was a captain for the past two consecutive years. During her free time, she enjoys reading, dancing, listening to music, and, of course, writing. Her goal is to major in English in college.

GRACE TWOMEY is a sophomore at Apex Friendship High School in Apex, North Carolina. She has won many schoolwide writing contests and has been published twice in *Saplings: The Carolina Young Artists' Magazine.* In 2012 Grace moved from New York to North Carolina with her parents, her younger sister, and her dog, Cocoa Puffs. In her free time she enjoys reading, playing guitar, and, of course, writing.

AMELIA VAN DONSEL is a senior at Waltham High School in Waltham, Massachusetts, where she is the editor in chief of her school's literary magazine. Her work has been on display several times at the U.S. Department of Education and published in numerous anthologies and magazines, including *The Best Teen Writing of 2015, The Best Teen Writing of 2016,* and American High School Poets National Poetry Quarterly as a national winning entry. She has also received gold medals and regional awards from the Scholastic Art & Writing Awards. After graduation, she intends to pursue a college degree in English and continue with her writing.

CPSIA information can be obtained
at www.ICGtesting.com
Printed in the USA
LVOW11s0008150617
538124LV00001B/154/P